Archie's Bunker

S oldiers are supposed to be battle hardened. Tough. They should be strong, resilient, and unaffected by emotions. But, when it comes down to it, they're human.

Inside a dark, dreary kitchen, I sat at an oak veneer, two-person dining table in a cracked vinyl chair, across from a balding, aged man who had seen the darkness humanity offers. He saw death, destruction, and chaos. As a reward for his bravery, he spent fifteen years after being discharged from the army seeing nothing at all.

How's that fair?

Sadly, fairness is not something most people find after a lifetime of sacrifice. For those who are wired to give of themselves to serve others, that isn't a deterrent. We just have to play with the hand we're dealt.

I know all about being dealt a less than savoury hand. But sometimes we sacrifice the things we want for the things we think are right.

"What are we having today, Finny?" Archie questioned, his voice weak and raspy. The last six months that passed, his lungs withstood several bacterial chest infections. With each one that went through his system, I convinced myself our visits would come to an abrupt end. This combat-hardened man continued to fight each bat-

1

tle, coming through the other side.

I had grown fond of him. A short, tubby man with a thick western accent. He lived a long life, a hard one at that, which was clear in his poor physical appearance and condition.

Not quite sixty, Archie was an old sixty. His body worn and his soul tired. He spent many years of his life alone. Convinced others wouldn't understand the way he worked. But I did, for the two of us were alike.

"Looks like we have corned beef for you today." I smiled as I placed the lukewarm meal beside him.

"How are you two getting on?" my mother's voice echoed from the kitchen. She was busy cleaning two weeks of filth that accumulated on the counter.

In Archie's depression, he let things slide. While he was blind, he always managed in his limited vision to keep himself clean and organised. When I first met him, his house was immaculate, but as I watched his mental health continue to deteriorate, so did the pride he once had.

I took it personally, always wanting to help Archie get out of his funk, but as my mother put it, it had to be up to him. I hated watching him continue to smoke, knowing that it was only causing him harm.

My mother told me I always had to set boundaries; something she was far better at doing than myself. As a nurse, she dedicated her life to helping others, always putting herself second.

I, on the other hand, even though I never expressed my emotions, had always been a fixer. Someone who wanted to assist others even when I couldn't assist myself.

"We are okay," I called back to her as I encouraged Archie to eat.

He paused; his empty gaze directed at me with mocked enthusiasm. "Hardly appetising there, Finn."

"I'm sure it's not as bad as you think."

"If you say so," he replied as he forced a heaped fork of dry corned beef and mashed potato down his throat.

"So have you gotten a lady friend yet?"

I laughed, knowing the very topic would have piped my mother's intrigue.

"Nay not yet Arch. Working on it."

That was a lie, I wasn't, but he seemed to find satisfaction in my white lie of searching for a soulmate.

"Hurry with it, would you? I want to give the lass my seal of approval."

I laughed with a nod. "All right, all right."

For the last year and a half, my mother and I spent a few hours every month volunteering for Blind Veterans in Scotland. For the life of me, I could never wrap my head around why my mother, who did nursing for a profession, would want to give up her spare time doing so. She seemed to love being around people, and despite my reluctance at first, I agreed to help her. She always expressed to me I would learn so much by doing so, and it was through Archie I came to understand her insistence.

Archie grew up in Aberdeen his whole life. From stories about the late sixties oil discovery in the North Sea to giving me a full understanding of Aberdeen's very own unique climate. The most important thing Archie would teach me would be how much I misunderstood my father.

My father was enlisted in the Navy and spent most of my life out at sea. He was based south at Her Majesty's Naval Base, Clyde, a three-hour drive from Aberdeen. While it would have been easier on us as a family to live in Glasgow, my mother hated the city.

We lived there for five years when I was a child before my mother was given a job opportunity in Aberdeen. She couldn't refuse and we relocated.

While my father was a soft-spoken man, my mother was the complete opposite. She graduated from nursing school when I was two years old. Initially, she started it before she got pregnant with me, but with my father away all the time and having little family support, she shelved it till she felt she could manage the workload.

Nobody believed she could do it, but she did. A testament to her work ethic. She would spend hours studying where she could and ended up passing with honours.

When my father returned home, he often struck me as odd. He wasn't the most engaging of characters, preferring to spend time alone. He seemed to hold a lot of devotions for my mother, but with me, often his affection felt forced.

As a child, I never understood until the summer of my fourteenth birthday, where I was assisting my mother and I met Archie.

Archie, who also served in the Navy himself, told me

not to take it personally. One day I had taken him out to his garden to feed the doves and out of nowhere, he made a statement that even after all this time has passed, I can't forget.

"When you spend so much time away from your loved ones, you become a different version of yourself."

Archie had three children that, in his older age, he was estranged from. Both of his daughters moved with their mother to America and his only son lived in Dundee, yet never visited him.

When I questioned him about it, his honesty always surprised me.

"I was a good soldier, Finn, not a good father. I pushed them all away, thinking they wouldn't understand what was up here," he said as he grasped his head.

"Don't make the same mistake I did by pushing others away. From what I can see, your father is a good father, even if neither of you two understand each other. You don't want to be me, Finn. If I teach you anything in life, let that be it."

At the time, I shrugged off his comments as nothing more than ramblings, but the more I focused on his little pockets of wisdom, I realised there was truth in his words.

He was right as the more time I spent with my father, the more I saw little parts of him I didn't even know were there. The layers of him are so fine that if you blinked, you would miss them. Even though he wasn't affectionate physically, he made his support known in other ways. From hours spent at football practice to taking me fishing when I knew he hated the idea. He tried his best, even if I wasn't able to see it. Where I thought he didn't love me, in his absence from our lives, I think distance grew between us and, as a result, the ability to know how to love me the way I needed him to as a child became foreign.

Perhaps that was my problem. I spent too much time alone and blamed him far too much for the failures in our relationship. As Archie said, too much time alone and you become a different version of yourself and, at some point, you have to take accountability for your share of the problem. The more time has aged me, I realise I have become further and further from who I thought I would be. Environmental or by personal action or choice, one thing was for certain: I was no longer the child I was.

As a child, I had always been a spirited kid with an appetite for life. My mother always used to laugh, convinced that I must have been on the attention deficit spectrum because of my inability to sit still. I never needed medication for it, but as I matured and life shaped me, it became more subdued.

I still had a hunger for adventure and spice in my life. It was just more manageable. That didn't change until I came back from my first deployment in the middle east. I did a tour in Bosnia previously, but it was on a mountainous range in Afghanistan, where my outlook on life changed.

When I arrived back on home soil, I became distant from everyone. With all that occurred on my deployments, each one took a part of me. I always feared losing the ones I loved after what happened to my brother, but when I lost close to two dozen people over five years, it put that loss on steroids, but not in the way I thought.

After Lyall, I always had an element of me that preferred not to get too close to others. But after what happened on tour, I distanced myself from feeling any sort of emotion at all. Not that I didn't want to feel it, but it became something I feared. While death didn't scare me, losing the ones around me did to the point I removed myself from becoming exposed to that vulnerability entirely.

I stopped caring about everything, including myself, and I was diagnosed with Post Traumatic Stress Disorder. While I came right after a year of intensive therapy, it became certain I would never be who I once was.

Even with my guard up, it seemed as if tragedy followed me no matter where I went. I lost two good friends to suicide within six months of returning from Afghanistan, which thrust me back to square one and derailed my efforts to move forward.

For some, they thought my emotional distance was because I didn't care, but I was always a reserved kid. One who always seemed to care too much, even when I didn't make it known. Ultimately, I just stopped expressing it and learnt how to dismiss my feelings. Problem is when you dismiss something so much, it is very hard to get it back. While I could still hold some degree of emotional vulnerability with my parents, for everyone else, I became a blank wall. I had to be to protect myself.

My best friend Blair always said to me I would have to let people in at some point, as life would become a lonely existence if I didn't. I never gave it much thought until I found myself forced to. The years I lost with my father, I couldn't change, but I could change the course of my life if I looked at the lessons from the mistakes we both made. I would be alone otherwise; alone in a world that didn't understand me just as much as I struggled to understand it.

Something I found out when my father was diagnosed with dementia.

Billy Elliot

The previous month was nothing short of tough. Dad had days where he would no longer eat. Days where he said nothing, alone in his inaudible silence. Other days, he only spoke in murmurs, unrecognisable noises, and grunts. Sometimes, he would entertain me for hours with stories of his naval adventures and childhood antics. No two days were the same and that became something I struggled with. The never knowing which version of my father I would face on any given day.

Since childhood, I had always been a creature of habit like my father. Someone who liked to know what the expectation of the day would bring and where the day would go. It only seemed a natural progression that I would follow my father's path to pursue a defence career in the British Army just shy of my seventeenth birthday. Much to my surprise, Blair joined me to cure his boredom and sudden declining grades.

Blair and I had known each other since we were kids. We grew up on the same street, three houses apart. After four girls, Blair's dad, the local mechanic, finally got the boy he'd always wanted. Despite everything, though, no matter what he did, Blair never met his father's macho expectations. A flamboyant redhead with a flair for dance, he became the closest thing to a brother I would ever have, and with four older sisters, I became the same to him. Often bullied growing up because of creative antics, everyone assumed he would become Aberdeen's very own Billy Elliot. Whilst Blair was soft-hearted, he was articulate. This made him a valuable soldier and an even more valuable friend.

When we both made the ultimate decision to enlist, it seemed nobody took him seriously, but no one less than his father. I remember the day as clear as crystal when we, after a day researching our options of trades, took it upon ourselves to tell our families of our intentions.

Blair went first. Standing behind him, I held my breath in anticipation. "Dad, I have something to tell you. I am going to join the army." The words spilled out of his mouth in a rapid, slurred fashion, as if he was so anxious, his mouth couldn't form the words.

His dad sat in silence, frowning, while he sipped on his lager in his infamous tatty brown recliner.

"Are you not going to say anything?" Blair blurted out after the lull in conversation became painful. His hands remained clasped behind his back like he was standing to attention, rocking slightly. There was a pause, both of us unsure where to look.

In response, his dad erupted into laughter, sending streams of beer foam through his nostrils. "Ye what now?"

I could feel the air fill with Blair's disappointment as I glanced over at his fidgeting hands. For as long as I had known him, he always yearned for a sense of approval from his father.

"I'm going to join the army," Blair said again, a bit more stern.

His father peeked at me before turning his attention back to Blair, studying him with a smirk. "Ye going to dance for them?" His dad laughed, slapping a hand on his thigh with a loud crack.

I knew Blair wouldn't retaliate. Not to his father, anyway.

"Let me guess, you are going to join them too, aren't ye chicken legs?" he said as he looked back at me. I stood tucked behind Blair, but his father was fixed on me with his dark eyes. I gulped, feeling uneasy under his scrutiny. I stared down at my rail thin legs, questioning if they would even support the weight of a pack.

His dad was always hard on him. I never understood his justification. Blair was the essence of a good person, worked hard and did no harm. He always sought to achieve good grades and always treated people kindly. But for whatever reason, he worked tirelessly for his dad's affections.

I remember I once questioned my father after Blair's dad picked us up from football practice when we were no older than ten. On the entire journey home, his father scorned him after he failed to defend a goal. My father never talked to me like that. Despite being a soft-spoken man, he had always given me support and guidance when he sensed I needed it. He told me that one day I would understand everyone has their own ways and styles in how they treat others. Still, I couldn't understand the dynamic between Blair and his father. I doubted I ever would. As I reflected upon it when I got older, that day

Blair told his father his plan to enlist marked the contrasted realities of our experiences growing up. That moment, for Blair, should have been a happy one, but there was little I could do as it became awash with resentment and disappointment. I realised then how fortunate I was.

His dad never took Blair's military aspirations with any element of seriousness, right until the day we left to go to basic training. As we boarded the bus to begin our new careers—our new lives—Blair's father said, "I'll see ye in two weeks, lad." His tone was joking, but his seriousness was evident. Blair shocked him and everyone else who doubted him when he became the top recruit through our basic training.

It was what I came to learn about Blair over our twenty-something year friendship, just how determined he could be. He always applied himself in every way, no matter the cause, always maintaining that if he didn't do his best, then it wasn't enough. I never understood whether his personality was to blame or whether he just wanted his dad to one day admit he was proud of him.

Me, I had always been a bit of a grunt, picking fights with those who questioned Blair's sexual orientation. It never seemed fair to me that people judged him so much. It was something he never, on the surface, seemed to care about. He never stopped his spirited dances, and he never retaliated, but knowing what I came to learn later in life, I suspected this had all been a facade.

Three weeks before *the* phone call, Blair visited Dad with me at the care facility.

When we arrived, Dad sat staring out the window in a bewildered gaze in the common room. I could tell he wasn't there with us that day, clear from his confusion as we pulled out our seats to sit next to him. Even though he had known my face over half his life, each day that passed, the familiar sense of me became more foreign.

"Dad, how are you?" I said as Blair turned his attention to one of the younger nurses deep in discussion with a lady two tables over.

Dad said nothing, scowling as he tried to piece the jigsaw of our presence together.

"It's Finn. Your son?"

The nurse who Blair fixated his attention on came over to us, giving us a jovial smile.

"He is having a bad day today. Aren't you, Mr McIntosh?" she asked, bending down to his eye level. "This is your son, Finn, and he has come to visit you today. Isn't that a delightful pleasure?"

Blair looked over at me in silence with widened eyes, as if to remark on the woman's attractiveness. Of short stature, strawberry blonde hair, and freckles, one could not deny she was attractive. I gathered she was from across the channel given her thick Irish accent, and even though she knew my name, I had yet to learn hers.

"I should probably introduce myself," she said, as she brought herself to a stand. "My name's Ainsley. I am going to be one of your dad's primary nurses from now whilst Sally is on maternity leave."

Sally had been Dad's nurse for the last year and a half but left to embrace motherhood. She and her husband conceived after multiple rounds of IVF treatments. She confided their fertility struggle with me once after a rough day early in Dad's diagnosis.

She was in and out of character when she tucked Dad into bed. I could see from her smudged makeup and un-enthused demeanour that something troubled her. After I asked her if she was okay, the floodgates opened, making the revelation known.

We developed quite a friendly relationship as time passed. She always remained professional, treating Dad in a way that allowed him to maintain his dignity and respecting his voice on days he had one. It was a natural progression since I saw her every weekend I was in town.

The day she told Dad and me their treatments were successful, she was expecting, Dad was lucid, aware of goings-on around him, and elated at the news. We both liked her. The epitome of a good person. Even as her patients swore and spat at her, Sally always did her best to remain upbeat.

When I met Ainsley for the first time, I found it humorous that the universe seemed to have taken an exact personality copy of Sally and placed it in a short fiery ginger with a pair of intense green eyes. She carried herself similar to Sally in the way she injected humour, speaking with such fluent vivaciousness. It was hard to ascertain if she even knew the emotion of anger.

"Nice to meet you, Ainsley," Blair said first, extending his hand.

"Are you the brother? A friend?" she questioned, with a lashing of curiosity in her voice.

"Aye, just a friend, but nearly brother, aren't ai Finn?"

"We have known each other since we were kids, and

he's still as much of a pain in my arse now," I joked, giving Blair a smirk.

She paused, checking her pocket before she pulled out a piece of paper. "Well, you have two visitors today. That is lovely, isn't it?" She gathered herself to continue her work, and I found myself not wanting her to leave. "I'll be back after my rounds. Have fun, you three."

Why did I feel relief knowing she'd be coming back?

She flashed us another smile before walking away, leaving Blair and I staring at Dad sitting in silence.

I missed him. It had to be one of the hardest things I have ever endured in life, watching his demise. A man who always was so meticulous about his presentation became unrecognisable. Studying his stained shirt and matted hair; it filled me with a sense of disconsolateness. It wasn't the nurse's fault for his unkempt appearance. He went through a phase where he was insistent on wearing the same shirt every day and bathing him became an issue. They did their best, but I couldn't shake the feeling I knew if Dad from twenty years earlier could see what had become of him, it would have caused him a great deal of despair.

"Are you all right, Finn?" Blair questioned as I continued to study Dad, deep in thought. I almost forgot Blair's presence with me as I lost myself in my desperate search of a sign Dad knew I was there.

"Aye, I am okay," I mumbled, turning my focus to him.

"That nurse seemed nice," he said as he raised his eyebrows, looking over my shoulder.

"You have a girlfriend. Need I remind you?" I replied

with a subdued laugh.

"I do not mean for me, you dafty. I mean for you."

My love life became quite the discussion between Blair and our other childhood friend, Colin. Both had been in stable relationships for some time, and I was last to get my feet on the starting line. Not that I was unattractive or uninteresting – not to sound cocky – but being in a relationship held no appeal to me. Letting someone in, being vulnerable; I didn't see the bright side.

Over the previous few years, I had several casual flings with women I worked with. The most serious being with a medic attached to our unit named Brianna.

Dating – a loose term for the casual arrangement we had while on deployment together – for a little over a year, Brianna and I developed a friendly relationship in Iraq. While initially it consisted of sexually charged banter, card games, and workouts, it developed into an intense friendship that soon led to friends with benefits.

The cause of our relationship's demise was ultimately my mistake. Or perhaps my unwillingness to give of myself what Brianna wanted from me. When we got home, she expected things to become official. After a year, she longed to label what we had. I thought she was happy with our casual arrangement, but she craved more, and I knew I couldn't give her what she desired.

At least in my immaturity, I thought I couldn't.

I heard from far too many people that once you label something, things change. I was happy, with no desire to share what we had with the world. We didn't have to be in each other's pockets, were able to fuck when we wanted, see each other whenever it was convenient. There was no need to ask questions or invade each other's privacy. It was simple. I liked simple.

I thought if we labelled it, there would be the expectation to have children. I wasn't ready to become a version of Colin and his wife Laurie, four kids in tow and never enough money.

Was it a mistake?

Possibly, but life goes on. A year later, Brianna was engaged to another guy from a different unit. They bought their first home together, while I spent most nights with my hand, playing far too much Xbox, occasionally looking her up on social media.

"I'm not looking for anything," I replied to Blair in a disgruntled tone. If I was to go looking for a relationship, it wouldn't be with my father's nurse.

"You're always going to be alone at this pace."

Maybe Blair was right, but why the emphasis on the idea that companionship meant happiness? I could never understand. I was happy, well – I certainly wasn't unhappy – and I met a lot of miserable people in relationships.

After a period of silence, Ainsley reappeared, peeked at the clock in a fleeting glance before she squared away the uneaten food on Dad's plate.

"Did you get anything out of him?"

"Not today," I replied as I brought myself to stand.

"Maybe tomorrow will be a better day?"

I knew I had to go back to my home in Edinburgh the

following evening, so I hoped she was right. I never enjoyed leaving him without the reassurance he at least had some recollection that I was there. It became a common worry that in his inability to remember, he would become lonely, or he would assume I didn't care. I watched the toll loneliness took on Archie, and I feared that for my father. The less coherent he became, the more this uneasiness grew. After losing my mother, I needed him in my life in ways he would never come to know. It was becoming clear, however, as each day passed, that time was limited, and I had no control over it.

A Changed Man

When I returned home from Afghanistan in the spring of 2006, my mother started noticing things in my father she thought were amiss. A man, once regimental in all areas of his life, became disorganised and chaotic.

As much as I wanted to, I couldn't give my father my full attention because, upon my return, I had my own issues to overcome. After my mother's bowel cancer diagnosis the Christmas prior, I didn't want to add to her stress, let alone my father's, so I battled in secret.

Six months later, I was diagnosed with PTSD, also known as post-traumatic stress disorder. I knew others who suffered – many who saw no way out but to end their life. I wanted more for myself, so instead, I committed myself to making my sole focus overcoming "The Darkness". As a result, in my effort to protect their high opinion of me, I lost time with both parents. It wasn't as if I saw myself as a failure. No, I just wanted to shield them from my turmoil; save them from the battle I brought home. I had always been stubborn – a trait I inherited from my mother – and believed I could get through it on my own. Being a lone wolf becomes a side effect of losing so many people close to you under tragic circumstances.

It took just over a year before I felt I could see my parents without fear of upsetting them. They didn't understand, but in my mind, they didn't have to, as it seemed to make perfect sense to me.

The Christmas of 2007, everything changed when my mother's prognosis became terminal. The changes within my father that, on all accounts, seemed like they were part of natural changes of age became something we couldn't deny any longer. I knew from my encounters with Archie, who was several years older than my father, that diminished memory was normal, but not to the extent my father displayed.

That weekend, I had gone home to see Mum as her oncologist advised us time was running out. The cancer had spread and there was little they could do. They expected she would have three to six months left to live, so from that weekend onwards, I tried to go home at every opportunity. She never dwelled on the fact she was dying. She confessed to me she accepted the moment they told her instead, and now the only thing she was worried about was how we would all cope in her absence.

The afternoon the severity of my father's illness came to a head. I had taken Mum out to the botanic gardens alone, finding a seat on a bench seat in the shade.

The once luscious auburn locks of hair my mother wore had become thinned by her recent rounds of chemotherapy. Even though we all suspected it wouldn't work, she insisted on the attempt to prolong her life, regardless. Of all the things she taught me in life, the most important was morality and choice. Till the day she died, she still carried herself in her way, with the elegance and flair that comforted me in all the storms of my life. Never one to complain, she was always more concerned about my father's changing health than anything else.

"Finn, I am worried about your father," she whispered, watching a pair of starlings dig in one of the flower beds.

"What do you mean you are worried?" I asked and turned to face her.

Grabbing my hand, she gave it a squeeze and took a deep breath. After a moment's silence, she said, "Finn, it's no longer just the keys or his wallet anymore. He is forgetting the simplest of things. On Monday, he was convinced Roger stole something of his from the attic."

She paused and her voice became tense. "I don't think he is very well."

Roger was our neighbour. After he lost his wife, Éloise, five years prior, he dedicated much of his time to assisting my father in building model boats. Roger never came to children of his own. I grew up to view him and Éloise, similar to an aunt and uncle figure. He and Dad were close mates and given Dad was quite an introverted and soft-spoken man, I was of the belief Roger was the only friend he ever had other than my mother.

"What do you think it is?"

She forced a nervous smile, picking at a loose thread at the bottom of her sleeve. "Finn, I think it's dementia. It must be. He has all the clinical signs... I..." she sniffed, pulling a hankie from her purse. "What am I to do? Finn, I feel so backed into a corner. He refuses to see someone, and it is getting worse."

In reassurance, I grabbed her hand, giving it a delicate squeeze. "It's going to be okay."

I knew nothing of dementia; Until I did.

When we returned to my childhood home that afternoon, I came to realise just how bad things were when my father insisted I was having an affair with his wife – my mother.

When we pulled up into the driveway, the door flung open.

"Who do you think you are?" he demanded, ushering my mother inside.

"Dad, stop!" I said, confused by his anger and hostility.

"Stay away from my wife."

What is he talking about? "Dad, stop and listen to yourself."

For a moment there was silence and then, as if something ticked in his mind, the anger on his face washed away. He continued to stare at me, dumbfounded by my startled expression, with neither of us sure of what to say.

"Finn, I'm confused... I..." he said after a moment, his voice trembling.

I glanced at Mum, supporting herself against the wall with tears smudged down her cheeks. She clung to the side of the house, appearing as though she'd collapse if she let go.

"Dad, it's okay," I mumbled as he ran his hands through his thinning hair.

I would come to learn that these episodes were becoming more frequent and with them also came aggression. Mum herself was deteriorating at an alarming rate and was in no position to deal with that on her own, even though she would try her best to. She did not have the mental or physical strength.

That afternoon when Dad was upstairs, I sat Mum at the dining room table and insisted that we put him into a care facility, to which she refused, as I suspected she would.

"I can handle it." She crossed her frail arms and narrowed her thinning eyebrows.

"Mum, absolutely not. No, you cannot. That..." I said, pointing upstairs. "That cannot be happening when I am not here."

"Finn, you don't understand. You don't know him like I do."

"The one thing I know, that was not my father. And you, you cannot be responsible for that."

Mum lowered her gaze, tears pooled in her eyes. "Finn, I'm dying. Nothing we do is going to change that. What you don't understand is I just... I just..." She lifted her gaze to look me in the eye.

"I just want to spend as much time as I can with him before I... before I go. You must understand that."

Whilst I was aware Dad had lost his bearings on things, I never realised it was so bad. Part of me was certain Mum chose not to tell me for that very reason. Even after three and a half decades together, they still loved each other. There wasn't a time in my life where I could ever doubt their affections for one another.

My mother always told me they balanced each other because they were so different, but one thing was for certain, they loved each other in every single meaning of the word.

I accepted her decision and dropped the matter. All I asked was that she promised to tell me if it got worse. She never got the chance. My mother died in her sleep two days later.

The day before she passed, we drove our Bow Fiddle Rock on the Moray coast. A place of significance. We scattered my brother's ashes there after he died nearly three decades earlier. Even though we never spoke about Lyall at length, the effects of his absence could be felt deeply rooted within all our lives. The only memory I recall of him lay in a faded picture of a chubby, smiling, blue-eyed infant, but for my parents, he was so much more.

I was three when he passed, but I remember the years of turmoil it placed on my mother afterwards. Her way of coping was to eradicate any memory of his existence. She ploughed on with life and threw herself into work, becoming a specialist in her field of paediatrics. She volunteered for various foundations, seeming to rationalise helping others as a way to make up for not helping Lyall. To many, though, it was evident that day, she changed.

Mum's sister, my aunty Agnes, expressed to me the day we lost Lyall, she lost part of her sister she never regained. I was so young; I remember Mum for the years after Lyall, but Agnes remembered how Mum was before that happened. It turned out they were quite the contrasting pair.

Agnes never had children of her own and I often spent a week of the school holidays with her. Alone, without the risk of another's ears, she took great pleasure in telling me stories of a side of my mother I never saw.

According to Agnes, my mother was once a vivacious woman who once dressed up as a man to make Agnes' ex-husband jealous after his year-long affair with his secretary. I saw nothing close to that side of my mother. She was always so serious, except for rare bouts of laughter and random public displays of affection with my father. With me, though, her heightened state of worry never took a break. On constant alert, she never relaxed, and as a result, I didn't either.

In her perpetual state of worry, she never became accustomed to me joining the military, even if that meant she had no control over my choices in life. It was as if she lived her life scared that she would lose me, and I often questioned how both of our lives could have been different if losing Lyall never happened. It became suffocating, particularly in my teenage years, where I felt I was granted no privacy. Always needing to know where I was and who I was always with. She always valued honesty and in return I was always an honest child, but as time went on, I lied to her in an effort to escape it all.

For my father, he hid his grief, and it wasn't until I was sixteen that I realised just how much the loss of Lyall affected him.

Shortly after my sixteenth birthday, I helped Dad paint the walls from their less than desirable yellow colour to a pastel blue. He disappeared into the attic for quite some time, and I went in search of him, concerned he had come to some harm.

"What are you doing?" I called out, hearing boxes shuffle across the floor from above.

"Aye Finny, just sorting things out," he called back,

popping his head through the access hole gap.

"I'm coming up," I said as I made my way up the ladder.

When I reached the top, I saw him bent over a rectangular box which contained several possessions that were once Lyall's. A small hand-crocheted teddy and blanket, several toys and outfits all crammed into a dark blue tote.

"Don't tell ye mother. I told her I threw these away," he said as he picked up a pale blue romper.

"I still think about him, Finny. It has been nearly three decades, but I still think about him."

I stood in silence, unsure of what to say as he pulled out each of the items inside, studying them before placing them in a small pile by his feet.

All our lives changed the day Lyall died, but it was in the attic I realised, for Dad, it would always be a lifelong void. While I wouldn't come to know until he was sick just how much he blamed himself for the events surrounding my brother's death, that day, as I watched him hold the remaining physical memories of Lyall's existence, I saw a part of his grief first hand.

He hid it so well, but in secret he found himself alone in the attic, having periodic moments where he clung to all he had left of Lyall. His smell may now have been replaced by the mustiness from the attic, but just the physical touch of something he once held dear seemed enough to bring him comfort.

Sometimes, he drove out to where we scattered Lyall's ashes, but Mum never had it in her to do the same. She knew where he was going and just accepted it was what he needed to do, but the day we took Mum there before she died, not going was a huge regret, she admitted.

It evades me why she wanted to go there that day after not being able to for the last thirty years, but part of me thinks she knew she was going to die.

For the first time since I was a child, we talked about him. Who he might have been and who he would have looked like. We laughed, and we cried all whilst the sunset painted the over the horizon.

With the last remaining light clinging on in the sky, my mother reached for my hand. I glanced at her with a smile, as she kept her view fixated out to sea. Of all the memories that became warped and disarrayed in her illness, I will never forget the way she looked that day. She was gravely unwell, but as the sun cast its glow on her pale skin, I caught the fleeting glimpse of the woman I remembered. The go-getter, firecracker, woman on a mission, never ceasing to try to make the world a better place. It would be the last time I would see her, dressed in her flowing, colourful dress, which hid her thinning limbs. Her face radiated with a smile; one I hadn't seen for some time.

"I am so proud of the man you have become, Finn," she whispered before she released my hand.

It would be the last thing she'd ever say to me.

A Promise To Myself

For reasons I still don't quite understand, after she told me, my mother delayed telling my father about her terminal illness for several weeks. When I questioned her about it, she told me I didn't understand, but one day hoped I would. Looking back, I think she knew full well the pain it would cause him and disclosed it while under the influence of a cocktail of morphine and sedatives. That way, her guilty conscience wouldn't be witness to the effect the news had on him.

Afterwards, I saw what she meant as it broke him. My entire life, I only witnessed my father cry a handful of times. That changed once she told him. A man who never expressed his emotions became one who must have cried for a month straight. A battle-hardened man, plagued with the human affliction: emotion. Upon my visits home, I often found him sobbing into items of my mother's clothing, lost in a trance of confusion knowing he was going to lose her. He remained helpless in his ability to stop that from happening. Despite his own illness taking its toll, knowing he was going to lose her seemed to be the one thing his brain wouldn't allow him to forget.

In its unfairness, life dishes out a fair helping of irony.

It seemed so cruel, to love someone the way he loved her, only to have to be in the passenger seat waiting for that life crash. I never wanted to love like that, let alone lose the way he was.

After her death, his illness progressed faster than I could have expected. Two weeks after my mother's funeral, I returned to work in Edinburgh. I had only been back two days when Roger called in the middle of the night and advised me my father was naked in the street, in the middle of winter, talking gibberish. When Roger told me he would monitor it, in my naivety I assumed it all would be well, and it was a one-off transgression.

A week later, that idea came to a crashing end when I sought a round-the-clock care giver after the third instance of him parading his nakedness around the streets of his small city. I got him two in-home carers, but it only lasted three days after he made inappropriate advances towards one of them. Completely out of character for him, he made me aware I no longer controlled the decision.

Blair volunteered to help me the day they put Dad into care. I didn't display emotions openly, but I couldn't contain them that day. After settling Dad into his room, I knew I would have to walk away, knowing his freedom was taken away because of me. Even though I knew I had no other reasonable course of action to keep him safe, I still felt overwhelming guilt and sadness for my part in the decision.

I mentally prepared all week for this eventuality in my head, but it soon became a realisation that no amount of planning could have made the transition any easier. The reality was so much worse than I expected.

Everything had gone well. My father appeared settled

and relaxed despite the change in routine. He seemed present, but also incoherent, clear in his periodic, slurring words about how much of a nice hotel it was. He didn't have full comprehension of his location or the purpose of him being there. I only hoped somehow he would understand in his own way.

Visiting time was nearing a close, and Sally entered the room to get him ready for bed, a pale-yellow gown and socks folded over her forearm.

"All righty," I said under my breath, preparing myself to stand. When my father saw me organising myself to leave, the tone in the air changed.

As Blair and I made our way towards the door, the room filled with a piercing shriek of panic from my father, one my ears had never heard before.

"Finn. Where are you going?" As if Dad connected the dots and knew what the future held, the calm I so naively thought would continue before the overwhelming emotional storm shattered. "Finn, please. Please don't leave me."

By that point, Blair stood in the hallway and cast a sympathetic stare in my direction. I froze as I struggled to find the ability to walk out the door.

I took a moment to glance at Dad, while tears streamed down my face. He began to throw his arms around, attempting to evade Sally, who, assisted by another nurse, did their best to hold him back.

"Finn, just go. We will be okay," Sally encouraged and gestured to me to go with her spare hand.

"Dad, I'm so sorry."

"Finn, please, I... I won't leave the house again. I just want to go home."

"Fuck," I muttered under my breath. His words pierced me, his desperation and panic coated in each word. I wished he could see I did this out of my love for him to keep him safe. If it was a matter of choice, I would have had it another way.

I glanced back to Blair again, who walked towards me. "Finn, just walk away."

I knew he wanted to offer encouragement, but I became immersed in my anger, as if they assumed the scenario playing out was easy for me. How could I walk away from my father who, at that moment, seemed inconsolable?

"I can't Blair. I can't fucking do it."

"You can do this. I know you know you can."

I took a deep breath, looking back at my father once more. "Dad."

"Finn, please," he wailed loudly, weakened from his attempts to free himself from their grip.

"I'm sorry, Dad. I love you; I love you so fucking much and I wish there was another way." I closed my eyes, which caused the water to break and sent a flood of tears down both cheeks.

"You've got this, Finn," Blair said, his voice just above a whisper.

I couldn't look at him, hiding behind the safety of my shut eyes.

At that moment, I wished I could convince myself of that. It seemed such an unattainable task, submerged in the guilt I was feeling.

Once I built the courage, I stepped into the hallway and allowed the door to shut behind me slowly. In the silence of the hallway, painted with the smell of pine disinfectant, I became overwhelmed with emotion.

"He's going to remember this. He is going to fucking remember this, Blair. And... he's going to hate me for it."

Blair shook his head, his eyes fixated in a condoling stare.

"Finny, he ain't going to remember this. He can't even remember this morning."

In my frustration, I got angry with Blair, throwing my wrath of my emotions in his direction. "What the fuck would you know? You can just fuck off... Just fuck off, would you?

"Finny, don't be like this."

"Please, just fuck off."

"Aye, as you wish." Blair bowed his head and gave me one last glance before he made his way down the hallway towards the glowing exit door to the right. "I'll wait for you in the car."

I glared at him, watching as he disappeared from view. I was left alone in the eerie silence of the hallway. I slid my back against the wall and brought my face into my hands as I started to sob.

Blair was right, because the more my father's illness progressed, the more he tended to live in his memories.

Often mixing them with the present, he would recall the happiest times in his life as if they just happened. Over the course of the week after his move into the care facility, I often found myself forced to relive what losing Lyall and my mother had been like for him; something that I never became immune to, no matter how many times he discussed it.

He asked for Lyall the first time a week before my mother passed. I was preparing dinner in the kitchen while Dad read a book in the lounge. Just as I was about to place the chicken in the oven, he leapt up from his chair in a state of panic.

"Lyall is due to wake up. I best check on him."

My mother laid in hospital struggling to breathe after deteriorating the night before. Given her condition, they felt it best to keep her in another day for observation. This left me alone to deal with a situation I had a scant idea of how to handle.

"Dad. Oh shit." I mumbled, before I placed down the knife in my hands and rinsed them.

"What is wrong with you?" he questioned, proceeding to look at me, confused. His hands remained gripped on the chair, arms in preparation to stand.

"Dad. Uh..." I sputtered, as I made my way towards him. Unable to find the words, my ears numbed with the loud thud of my heart racing.

"Finn, what's wrong?"

"Dad, I'm sorry, but Lyall died. He died when I was just a toddler."

He paused, holding his confused expression as he

tried to piece together the words that came from my mouth.

"What are you talking about? Finn, I just put him down for his sleep."

He shook his head and shot up to stand. Before I had time to stop him, he made his way up the stairs, leaving me with no choice but to follow him.

"Dad, please listen," I begged in desperation, doing my best to grab his hand before he reached the top of the stairs. He stopped before he took an instinctual turn to the left to what was Lyall's bedroom. He glanced at me for a minute before he turned the handle.

"Finn, you're acting ridiculous. He's right in..." He opened the door to find the room barren minus several miscellaneous items that wouldn't fit in the attic. "He... was... he was in here." In his panic, he couldn't comprehend the situation. "Finn, I... Where is he? Where is my son? What have you done with him?"

"Dad, I'm sorry."

Frantic, he opened every single door in a frenzied search of the child he remembered in his mind.

"Dad, he is not here. Please stop this."

I felt desperate. Tears welled in my eyes. I could do nothing but follow him in his state of confusion and search every room.

"Finn, he is here. He was right here," he insisted.

"Dad, please." Seizing an opportunity, I grabbed his hand as he walked past me before he could enter the bathroom, the last of the rooms he had left to check. "Dad, you need to listen to me. Lyall is dead. He is not here, he never was. You need to trust me. He died many, many years ago."

After a brief glance in my direction, studying my solemn expression, and his eyes widened as he realised I spoke the truth. "Oh god, Finn. What is happening to me?"

He dropped his gaze to his feet, his skin shaded in its greyish pallor. The anxious, defiant expression decorated on his face changed to sorrow as he cried.

"I don't understand, Finn. I don't understand."

"Come here," I said, my voice no louder than a whisper. As I brought him into my arms, his whole body trembled from the revelation. The sensation overwhelmed me and caused the flow of tears to quicken and my stomach to knot.

Of all the things the illness took from me for my father, the hardest had to be the one to make him relive his grief.

Lyall became a common fixture in our lives in several ways. Dad often made multiple purchases online to prepare for his arrival, leaving me having to return everything in a state of embarrassment or donate what could not be returned. I didn't have power of attorney, so I held no authority to cancel his cards. Eventually, I just hid them in places I knew he would never look. The insides of shoes, behind picture frames, and pots and pans. Each time he believed he lost one, he would order another, and the cycle continued. He rang people he hadn't spoken to in years to let them know he was having another son and even went so far as to put a birth announcement in the paper.

Whilst most people understood, I still sensed everywhere I turned, people would talk about it. I wanted to escape as it became something I struggled with. What hit me heaviest, however, was having to tell him about Mum.

The day I reminded him about Mum for the first time, I had taken him out for brunch about a week before he went into care. The whole morning, he was in good spirits, chatty and happy.

That all changed when he saw her, a woman who posed a striking resemblance to my mother before she became sick.

The woman took a seat three over from us with her husband and what appeared to be her adult daughter. I sat and watched Dad's face change in a rapid, dramatic fashion as he kept his eyes steady in their direction.

"What is she doing?"

I glanced over at where he was staring, his eyes fixated in a displeased glare.

"What is who doing?" I questioned him as he appeared to become angrier by each passing minute.

"Your mother. How could she be so disrespectful?" he hissed, placing down his knife and fork.

My heart sank as I realised what so far been a pleasant morning would change for the worse. "Dad. It's not Mum. Please calm down."

"For crying out loud, Finn. I am well aware of what my wife looks like."

I could see he was in the preparation to stand and

given how loud his voice had become, attention was fast being drawn to us; attention neither of us needed.

"Dad, sit down," I said in a stern tone. "It is not her."

"Yes, it is. Are you in on this too?"

What on earth is he talking about? In on what?

I scanned the crowded eatery, my nervousness growing from all the eyes on us.

"Dad, stop this! Mum died over a week ago."

I grabbed my mouth, realising what I just said, hearing several gasps from the patrons who were a captive audience to the situation at hand.

Dad paused, turning his head to face me in slow motion. "No..." There was the faintest tremble in his voice as he tried to digest the words.

"Dad, she was sick. She was very sick for quite some time."

"But she..." he pointed over to the woman, trying to make sense of the situation becoming unravelled.

"It's not her. I can take you to her, I can show you if you like."

He nodded in reply, and in silence I escorted him away from our table, leaving our half-eaten breakfast for the taking.

We drove in silence to the cemetery, a mere seven-minute drive from where we were. Once we were standing over her recently churned grave, still yet to have its headstone, he broke down to his knees, running his hands through the upturned dirt.

"This can't be so," he wailed, his cries echoing around us.

I stood several metres back behind him, watching as he leaned forward, smoothing the dirt with his hands. A sight even to this day that I cannot shake, a sight which, unbeknown to me, would come to happen again and again.

Losing my mother had been one of the darkest days of my life, and I became forced to relive that exact day.

That night after I dropped him back at the facility, I drove back to Mum just to be alone with her. I needed her more now than ever. I needed her advice on how to deal with this. I did not know what I was doing. In my desperation, I held onto the hope that she would be there that day. Perhaps she could somehow tell me what I needed to hear. But, that night, the air was filled with silence minus the bustle of the breeze churning the leaves that decorated the ground.

"Mum, I need you," I whispered. "I really need you."

Going Home

In all that happened since my return from Afghanistan, my year's absence before my mother's passing weighed on my mind. My condition caused both of my parents endless worry, but I didn't want to burden them, particularly her, with the demons I battled when she was dealing with her own. Talking about my life with the psychiatrists the Army provided was hard enough – let alone my mother. I knew she would never have judged me, but it felt easier to keep my distance. It destroyed me inside that the cancer robbed us of her before we had the chance to reconnect. Before I had the chance to explain why I disappeared.

In the weeks following the funeral, I spent a lot of time reflecting on all the words I'd left unspoken to the woman who not only gave me life, but loved me so unconditionally, even when I didn't deserve it.

The day of her funeral, nothing could have prepared me for what would unfold. The morning before the service, my father spent most of his time gazing out the window at the snow falling from the silver sky. Though the winter had been mild, that day, there were light snow flurries falling in the city. My mother always loved the snow, so the very sight was comforting.

I let him be, forming the assumption he didn't want to talk about his thoughts. Who could blame him for that? The hardest thing was, I knew he didn't comprehend the situation, given his constant loop of repetitive questions. It was the first time I would come to realise just how much his memory had faded. In contrast with Archie, who, even with his bouts of depression, remained quite sharp. My father could recount a lot of his childhood memories. It was the present which came few and far between.

After I showered and changed, I made my way downstairs. For the third time that morning, my father questioned if my mother was ready yet.

"Dad..." I paused, taking a deep inhalation of breath, then knelt to meet his gaze.

"Dad, today we have to say goodbye to her."

"Goodbye to who?"

He looked at me with a scowl and for a moment I stared at him, into his eyes. In their wide, confused glare, I tried to find him, knowing wherever he was, he wasn't here. "Please, not today," I murmured, feeling frustrated he no longer made the choice. My lips trembled under the weight of my building emotion. Of all the days, I wished he could just be himself and not be dissociated. Ma's funeral was that day.

"Dad, Mum, she died. Today, well, today we need to say goodbye."

A moment of silence passed as he struggled to process what I said before he broke out into heavy sobs. All I could do was hold him, knowing nothing would ease the pain of knowing he lost the love of his life.

"How many times have we had this conversation?" he

asked once he could stem his emotions.

I gulped, feeling a dryness in my throat. He knew in his lucid moments that things were changing, but struggled to understand the complexity.

"Three times," I said under my breath as I straightened his tie.

I relayed that exact conversation three times with him over the course of the morning, and it got no easier. Each time, I would tell him, he would break down, then after a short time, forget the conversation had ever taken place.

We kept the service small, two dozen or so. A handful of friends my mother worked with and what little family I had. My dad's older brother, Neville, who lived up in the Shetland Islands and his wife, Carly, who I hadn't seen since I was a teenager, and my dad's sister, Leslie, were also in attendance, much to my surprise.

Leslie and my father spent most of their adulthood estranged, for reasons I didn't come upon till my twenties. She battled addiction issues for quite some time and when my father's mother, Anne, died, I came to learn Leslie gambled and devoured all of Dad's inheritance in her addiction. She had been sober for the last five years, but my father never forgave her.

Barely recognisable, dressed in a tailored suit with her blonde hair tied back in a tight ponytail, it took me a moment to recognise her as she walked towards us.

"Finn," she said before she gave me an affectionate hug. She glanced at my father with anticipation in her eyes, but he kept his gaze fixed to the ground.

"Brother," she mumbled, not willing to let the moment pass without his acknowledgement. "How is he?" she queried, her attention turned back to me, given my father's displeased silence.

"Not great. Things are happening very quickly. Quicker than I thought."

"What will happen now?"

"He will be, well, he will go home in the next few days."

She nodded; her eyes glistened from impending tears. "Is there anything I can do?"

"Yes, you can stay the hell away from my family."

"Dad!"

"Finn, this woman is disgraceful. She shouldn't even be here."

I stared at him dumbfounded as Leslie said nothing, pursing her lips together before excusing herself.

"Did you really have to do that?" I hissed once she was out of audible range.

"I will not have that woman come and prey on you," he shrugged before disappearing back into his own world again.

One thing I came to learn quickly as his illness progressed was that he became quite obnoxious and forthright with his thoughts. He was always such a quiet man, one of little worlds and confrontation, yet as time passed, his outbursts became challenging. Two weeks before my mother's death, I took him out shopping and in the local butchery he became impatient with the queue, releasing profanity on the unexpected patrons. I never told my mother. I could tell she had enough worry as it was, but somehow, given her surprise when I suggested taking him out, my guess was she had already become witness to such an outburst.

"You ready?" Blair questioned, walking over to us.

I nodded, taking my father's arm before we headed inside the church.

One of my mother's work colleagues, Jennifer, talked first. They went through nursing college together and my mother spent most Friday nights at other's houses, drinking red wine to 80s love ballads.

"Bonnie and I met on the first day of nursing college. I was crying, because, as many of you know, I had just gone through my divorce. I never dealt well with change, and it was one of the scariest moments of my life. Bonnie marched right up to me and took my hand. 'Don't worry,' she said. 'I'll take care of you.' That's the kind of person she was. She was always the person who would step up and take care of someone sad or hurt or afraid."

She took a deep breath as she smiled in my direction.

"That's why none of us were surprised when she moved up the ranks. On the worst day of people's lives, she was there. She was willing to put herself on the line to protect people and their families. In the end, she continued to save people right until she died, and she wouldn't have had any regrets about that, so I can't either. I'm still sad about it though as we promised each other we would still drink red wine in the old folks' home. I love you forever Bonnie, I'm so blessed our lives crossed."

Jennifer paused again, looking down at the podium before clearing her throat as she wiped a tear from her eye.

"Finn," she said, her eyes fixed on me, "she was so proud of you. Every day you were overseas, we would watch the news together, hoping you were okay. We both worried about you. She always maintained you were the biggest accomplishment in her life and anyone who spent five minutes in a room with her knew it."

My father sat in silence the whole time, picking at a loose thread on his blazer while I sat rigid, trying not to break down. When it was time for my eulogy, I tapped his arm to get his attention.

"Dad, are ye going to be okay with Blair and Colin while I go up?" I whispered, to which he nodded in reply.

Standing at the podium, I felt my eyes become watery as I stared down at the three rows of sparsely populated benches. I glanced over towards Blair and my father, who hadn't changed his position, keeping his gaze fixed to the floor.

"Thank you to everyone for being here," my voice croaked as I did my best to soothe the dryness in my throat.

"Today we are here to celebrate, remember, and honour my mother. What can I say, what a great woman she was. After she passed, I realised how grateful I was to have spent hours on end with her during the final chapter of her exceptional life. My mother worked hard throughout her life, sometimes 50 or 60 hours per week. No matter how tired she was, she would always come home with a smile. I have never met someone who just seemed so happy to be alive – content with a simple life, helping others. My mother brought her limitless knowledge and tender humility and care to every task at hand. Her co-workers described her as a silent powerhouse; the type of person who would keep working after everyone left. Even when she became sick, she never complained. Even when it was becoming clear that she was in pain, my mother remained quiet and true to each task."

I paused, glanced over in Blair's direction to see he was struggling with my father, trying to keep him seated.

Not today. Please, Dad.

"Where am I?" my father called out, his words echoing from all four walls of the church.

I panned the room, the air becoming filled with curious whispers. Blair was doing his best to ration with him to calm down, but I sensed it wasn't going to be simple.

"Excuse me," I said, humiliated, my voice no louder than a whisper.

I made my way down the stairs to my father, now standing, doing his best to ward off Blair's grip.

"I'm sorry, Finny," Blair said, with a remorseful expression spread across his face.

"Dad, please stop," I said. I tried to grab his right arm to calm him, but he pulled it back in defiance.

"Finn, where are we, and who are these people?"

I closed my eyes for a moment, doing my best not to break down.

"Dad, please, can we not do this now?"

"Where are we?"

"Dad!" I found myself unable to prevent myself from becoming angry.

"Please, can you just sit down?"

He looked at me, studying my face before he peered over my shoulder at the casket placed next to the podium.

"Who died? Where is your mother?"

His tone became panicked as he searched the small crowd of faces for her familiarity.

"Where is your mother, Finn?"

I couldn't answer him. In my peripheral, I could see Blair, perplexed by what to do.

"Finn, where is she?"

"Come outside with me," Blair said, in my silence trying to coax my father outside.

"Get your hands off me."

Taking a deep breath, I knew there was nothing I could do but tell him the truth. I wanted to protect his privacy. I wanted to hold on to his humility, but I had no choice.

"Dad, Mum is gone."

"I don't believe you. Is that her?" he said, infuriated.

"Why would I lie to you?"

"Show me! You show me it is her."

Please don't do this. Come back to us, Dad.

"I am not showing you. Dad, stop!"

"I will get everyone out of here," Blair said, moving past us and ushering everyone outside.

"Show me."

I watched as the church emptied in a single file with the odd whisper of confusion.

"Okay, I'll show you," I murmured.

I had seen people in caskets before but somehow found the idea of seeing my mother in one an idea I didn't want to entertain. Blair encouraged me to see her before the service, but in my mind, I didn't want it to be my last memory of her. A choice I thought should have been mine to make now became one I was forced to change. In silence, we made our way over to her, pausing before she came into view.

I closed my eyes, unable to look as my father's cries erupted through the church. In the background, 'Going Home' played along to the flashing video montage from the projector.

"When Finn? When did this happen?"

I held my eyes shut in silence, wanting to make the moment stop, but I knew that was not possible.

"When Finn? When did this happen?"

"Two days ago, Dad. She was sick. She was very, very sick."

I opened my eyes as I watched him bent over her, stroking her face.

"Why can't I remember? Finn, why can't I remember?"

"Dad, you..." I walked over to him, staring down at my mother. Dressed in a white silk dress with an auburn wig that matched her own hair before she had become sick, she looked like she was asleep.

"She looks beautiful," I whispered to him, wrapping my arms over his shoulders. "She loved you, Dad. She loved you, and she was a very sick woman."

"Why can't I remember, Finn?"

"Because, Dad. You are very sick too."

Questions and Answers

When I had to get my father assessed for his care requirements two days after my mother's funeral, they questioned when we first noticed symptoms. Initially, it started off with forgetting names of people he had known his whole life, repeating himself during conversation and losing his way around the house. Three days after the incident with Roger, I awoke that Saturday morning to my mother crying in the bathroom.

"Mum," I mumbled with a gentle tap on the door.

"Finn, not now, okay?"

I peered through the crack in the door, watching as she bent over the sink, still wearing her nightgown. She was losing weight rapidly, her skin tainted with a soft yellow jaundiced tone. Her oncologist queried if we wanted her to go into palliative care, but she refused, ever the defiant woman, she didn't want her independence robbed.

"Where is Dad?"

She paused, staring at her reflection, unaware I was watching her. She looked drained, her heart heavy with sorrow.

"He is downstairs, Finn, " she mumbled, still staring at her reflection.

"I'll meet you downstairs."

For a moment, I watched as she closed her eyes. It was a memory I will never forget. The way she looked, the way she sobbed. I knew she was breaking despite putting on a brave face. She had been withholding her medication, concerned it would make her too incoherent to be aware of my father's forever changing behaviour, but I could see her fighting the pain.

Downstairs, my father sat on the couch and stared out the window, fidgeting with his hands, talking to himself in short, delirious mutters.

"Morning, Dad."

"Finn," he said, his voice sombre.

"Everything all right?" I questioned, pausing in the doorway between the kitchen and the lounge.

He shook his head, picking at his thumb. "She hates me."

"Who hates you?"

"Your mother."

"She doesn't hate you. Don't be daft."

He glanced up at me, his eyes pained with guilt. "Finn, I am forgetting everything. What if I forget her?"

I froze. It was the first time, by his own admission, that he knew the tides were turning.

"You won't forget her."

"I seem to forget everything else. I forgot where the bathroom was. Finn, I forgot where the bathroom was. The bathroom, of all things."

He shook his head. "She didn't ask for this."

"No, I didn't, but I didn't ask for cancer either," my mother interrupted from behind me. "Everything is going to be fine," she said, giving my shoulders a gentle squeeze.

"Can I have a moment, Finn, in the kitchen?" she whispered.

She shut the door behind us, biting her lip and directing her eyes towards the cabinets. "Finn, I know what you are going to say but –"

"Hang on. He said he forgot where the bathroom is?" I questioned, interrupting her.

For the first time in my life that I could recall, she raised her voice at me. "Finn, no. Stop right there. Everything he is experiencing is normal."

"You haven't even had him diagnosed yet!"

"Clearly I don't need to," she fired back.

"He needs to go."

"Need I remind you, Finn, whilst you were doing what you felt you needed to do for months on end, it was me who was here. You cannot walk into this situation thinking you know what is best when you were not here." She grabbed a glass from the top right corner cupboard, slamming it on the counter before she reached for the bottle of whisky to the left. I stared at her, unable to retaliate, knowing what she said was true.

"Finn." She shook her head twice before pouring herself a drink. "I shouldn't have said that. I'm sorry."

"Mum, it's only ten in the –"

"I realise this," she snapped before downing her glass.

I watched in silence as her hands gripped the edge of the counter. Her arms trembled under her own weight, although she now weighed less than eight stone.

"Finn, I haven't got long. I feel it." She murmured, breaking the silence.

I paused, staring at her, confused. "What do you mean you haven't got long?"

She poured herself another drink, tears streaming down her cheeks. "I feel it. I can't describe it to you, I just know." She finished her second drink and took a deep, rattled inhalation of breath. "Finn, do what you want with him when I am gone from this world. But I will not lose him before I go. You hear me? I can handle it."

In my mother's attempt to handle the situation, as she called it, I questioned if it had done more harm than good.

Two days after her funeral, I found myself with my father in our local doctor's practice, where they asked us to describe what was going on. That day, I learnt just how little my mother shared with me, whether or not that had been my doing.

My father was quiet as the doctor questioned me over and over, trying to build a timeline of events. After my year's absence when I hid in Edinburgh, I only visited home in my pockets of leave and the occasional weekend. I was only privy to so much from what I observed and what limited information my mother provided me. Just as I was about to reiterate that morning, my father reached into his pocket.

"I have an exact timeline," he whispered before thrusting the piece of paper across the desk.

The doctor glanced at me before turning his concern to my father with a perplexed stare. "Who wrote this?"

My father paused as he closed his eyes. "My wife did."

The doctor unfolded the piece of paper, taking a moment to read it before placing it down. "Was she in the medical field?"

"Yes, she was a nurse."

"That makes sense," he said, proceeding to tap his pen on his desk.

I would come to learn my mother had noticed things for a little over three years. It started with his keys after always putting them in the same place for all my life. Then, he forgot when he paid bills, often paying them two to three times over. What I thought only started a year prior was, in fact, three years. Three years in which my mother fought this battle in secret. It appeared we were each trying to save each other from heartache and turmoil, but little good it did for any of us.

While in Afghanistan, she often wrote and made small revelations of certain instances but never in a direct context. I wondered if that was a way to protect me or whether it was a way of protecting herself. My absence in the twelve months that followed my return did little to improve my knowledge of the situation, but in hindsight, would it really have made a difference? I couldn't take care of myself in those moments, so I would have been of little use to her.

After we left the doctor's surgery that morning with a referral for a scan and blood tests, I sat in the car with my father again absorbed in his world of scrambled thoughts and memories.

"Dad," I said to get his attention.

I wanted to know why she hid it from me and if he had known, but I knew just by his expression on his face, it was something he wasn't in the mood to visit that day.

"Never mind," I muttered, before turning the key in the ignition.

Two days later, I found myself back at the clinic, staring at the same four walls, only this time I felt a sense of comfort knowing at least the questions that plagued his behaviour would get answered in certainty. I received a call from one neurologist, Dr Wells, that morning requesting to see me. My father had his series of tests only that morning, so I was surprised he wanted to discuss with me so quickly.

As I scanned the room of half a dozen unfamiliar faces, a woman perked my interest. I could tell I was not the only one. She looked in her late forties, dressed in formal corporate wear with a layered platinum bob haircut. I sensed her nervousness as she clung to an elderly woman's hand, reminding her several times where they were. I could see by the fourth time her frustration was building, evident in her scowl and several loud exhalations of breath. There was familiarity in her body language, with each nervous scan of the room, each dashing glance at the clock. I understood it, for it was something I experienced myself. Her face wore the same exhaustion, pain and sadness I became accustomed to wearing. She caught my gaze briefly, smiling, before turning her attention back to the elderly woman seated to her right.

Fifteen minutes later, I looked up to see a tall, clean shaven, dark-skinned man with his hand outstretched as he crossed the room.

"Dr Wells, hi," I said as I stood to shake his hand. I realised he was who I had spoken to on the phone by his name tag sewn onto the left breast pocket of his coat.

"Follow me, we will use my consultancy room," he said, walking towards several rooms next to the day ward reception desk. We entered a small room with two chairs facing a mahogany L-shaped desk with several pictures of the brain and some thought-provoking quotes on the wall. "Take a seat."

I pulled out the chair closest to the door, sinking into its light brown leather fabric, watching as he studied the notes on his desk.

"All right, where do I begin?" he said out loud, flicking the pages to study his scan results once more. He cleared his throat, lifting his gaze to meet my own. "Finn, I'll be honest with you first and foremost. Your father's weight concerns me. He weighs less than nine stone and refuses to eat food. At this rate, we are going to have to sedate him to get a feeding tube in him to prevent him from deteriorating further." He picked up another piece of paper from his file and slid it towards me. "This is his CT from yesterday." He tapped a patch on the image, darker than the rest. "I know there was a suspicion of potential Alzheimer's disease, and this confirms it. You can see here, clear in these dark patches. It is quite profound, so he is in an advanced stage of the disease. So much so, I am surprised he has managed at home so well without needing care yet."

"My mother was very stubborn." I muttered under my breath.

"Where it is dark, you can see the excessive proteins. These become toxic to the nerve cells in the brain and the nerve cells start dying. These dying nerve cells are removed by the body as they are not useful anymore, leaving gaps in the brain tissue. Because of the gaps left behind by the dead nerve cells, the overall brain tissue shrinks." He pointed again to three large black masses illuminated on my father's scan. "This was more than I expected."

"What is his long-term prognosis?" I questioned, my gaze fixed on the clock behind him, desperate to prevent myself from falling apart.

"Not good. We will do our best, but it's not just his brain that is going. His kidneys aren't looking great based on his bloodwork. I think we are looking at weeks."

I brought my right hand to my forehead, grabbing the fold of skin between my fingers with a pinch. "Oh man," I replied, my voice nearly inaudible. He said the words I suspected were coming but didn't want to admit, let alone hear.

"He is comfortable at the moment, Finn. That is all that matters for now. We will look after him the best we can, but I feel it would be ill advised not to tell you to prepare yourself that once you get to this stage, the downhill slide can be rapid and exceptionally hard."

I nodded, unsure of what to say as his gaze stayed

fixed on me.

"I will let you see him now. We will organise to get him transferred onto the ward while you get your affairs in order."

"Thank you," I breathed, as I stood on my feet.

"Finn." He paused, giving me a sympathetic look before he shook my hand. "I see people in here all the time going through exactly what you are, and I always tell them just as I am going to tell you." He grabbed a pamphlet from a line of brochures decorating the wall to the right of the exit door. "It is going to get worse before it gets any easier, and I can highly recommend the organisation here who offer counselling and a friendly ear."

Great, he thinks I need a shrink; I thought as I took the brochure from his hands.

"Often people don't invest in their own mental health during this time, which I know is probably very overwhelming. The best piece of advice I can give you having gone through losing both my own parents is don't leave it till it's too late."

He studied the brochure list once more, grabbing another, second from the right.

"Look after yourself, Finn. The road ahead isn't a pleasant one."

An Unlikely Friend

T he transition into the home didn't go as easily as I expected. Some days were easier than others, but after a week of bad days, I became drained. It was hard not to find myself frustrated at the situation. I was succumbing to pressure, knowing that I only had three days left of leave before due back at work. I exhausted all my financial resources getting my father organised, as it would take months for my inheritance from my mother to take effect. The house needed work. I couldn't fathom selling it, but I knew I didn't have a choice. I could not afford Dad's care without doing so, regardless of how long he had left.

The morning I met Ainsley for the second time, I felt overwhelmed. Making my way down the narrow hallway mixed with the smell of disinfectant and mints, I suddenly heard my father when I reached the door three down from him.

"Get away from me," he said, voice saturated in panic. As I reached his door, I watched as he backed himself into the corner closest to the window, swaying on his feet. His mobility worsened faster than I thought it would, and he struggled just to hold his balance when standing. Defiant, stubborn in his ways, he did his best to try.

"Come on now, we need to give you a wash and get you organised for the day." I stood silently in observance as Ainsley, no bigger than five feet tall, did her best to bring him down from his heightened state. "Come on," she said, her voice firm, patting the bed with her right hand.

Dad glanced at me standing in the way, his face calming slightly as if he knew my face, but the pieces didn't connect. "Sir, can you please help me? I do not know this woman. I do not know her," he said, his voice weak and trembling.

Ainsley spun around to see who Dad was talking to, unaware of my presence. "Hi," she said, her face tinged pink but displaying a welcoming smile.

"Hi?" I said with a laugh.

"Finn, right?"

"Aye. Amy?"

"No, Ainsley," she corrected, leading Dad back to his bed gently.

"Ainsley, that's right, my apologies," I said as I entered the room, placing my brown paper bag of groceries on the floor.

"None needed, I get it all the time."

There was a moment of silence as Ainsley turned her attention back to Dad, and I made my way around to his side of the bed.

"Dad, be nice to the poor girl, would you?" I joked, given it was clear it was not going too well for either of them at that point.

"Finn?" Dad questioned; his expression more relaxed. I got a fleeting sense of hope he was aware of who I was, but I should have known better than to assume.

"Aye, that is the one! You remember now. That is always a good sign."

He shook his head. "I'm sorry I don't have a son called Finn. My son is called Lyall. I think you are in the wrong room."

I glanced across the room towards Ainsley, who looked at me sympathetically in response. I froze, unsure how to explain it to him in her presence. Before I could correct him, he smiled. "He is coming soon, you will see." I held my breath as I watched him smile with such certainty in his belief. As quickly as it had begun, the moment passed. Shifting his gaze out the window, he fell back into his own world, leaving what I said undigested.

"Great," I muttered under my breath, which Ainsley overheard.

"It is always hard when they get to this stage," she turned to me and said softly, filling up a small rectangular wash basin.

"Have you done this long?" I inquired, given she seemed so relaxed about the situation.

"Me? No, a little over two years."

"You seem so confident."

She laughed as she wrung out a flannel. "The trick is, you have to let them think you are in control. A lot of the time you're not because they aren't either."

"Well, that is one way to look at it."

"I enjoy my job. You know, you think they aren't aware, but I see pockets of awareness. Sometimes they can't communicate it so readily, but the brain is an amazing thing. I always try to maintain humour, otherwise this place can get overwhelming."

I nodded in reply, pulling the singular chair next to my father's bed towards me to take a seat. "I can imagine it is a thankless task."

"I think you are in the wrong profession if you think in nursing, you get thanked. A lot of the time I just get spat on and yelled at. Certainly, has given me an appreciation for good manners," she said with a grin.

"No." I laughed at her unexpected frankness.

"All the time. Makes me feel alive."

"Alive?"

"Well, what else can make you feel more alive than that?" she questioned jokingly, wiping Dad's face clean.

"I can think of a lot of things."

She smirked. "I'm sure you can." She kept her attention on me, pulling a pair of socks over Dad's legs as he stared at the ceiling, talking in faint mumbles. "So, Finn, what do you do?" Her lips turned up slightly at the corners, but I couldn't read the intent behind it.

"What do I do?"

"For a job. What makes your life riveting?"

I hesitated, amused by her humour. "I am in the army and riveting? Well, that is certainly not the first thought that comes to mind."

"Really? Army? Wow, okay. Can't say I have met an army man before. I should've guessed by the hair."

"What is wrong with my hair?" I question, running my hands over my patchy, number two haircut.

"It is, well, short."

"It usually is shorter."

She looked at me in disbelief, smirking.

"I somehow doubt that it could be any shorter than that. Tell me, do you enjoy it?"

"I guess, eventually I will get out and do something else."

"What do you want to do?"

"I'm not sure at this point. I assumed it will eventually come to me, but I'm still waiting for that to happen."

"You are never too old to switch careers. I was the oldest in nursing school by a mile and a half."

My mother always told me women are driven by curiosity and hold a sense of mystery. It was something I never forgot, and something I found to be true in my limited experience with women. I smirked, the thought fresh in my mind of my mother's words, realising the one-sided nature of the conversation. I'd told her a lot about myself but learned almost nothing about her.

"You hardly look old."

I studied her, trying to establish her age. She tied her red hair back in a bun and applied a light layer of makeup to disguise the freckles I had seen the first time we met. She looked to be in her late twenties, I guessed.

"I consider thirty-two fairly old when you are surrounded by twenty-year-olds," she retorted.

"Well, I am thirty-three. Does that make you feel younger?"

She laughed at my admission, bending underneath the bed to check his catheter bag.

"Well, yes. Yes, that does. How does it feel being so old?"

Blair was right. She was attractive. I unintentionally thought as I mused over her humour. More than just her external appearance. I enjoyed her presence, her laugh, her philosophies.

"Well, I can tell you it is all downhill from here." I said, as I mulled over her intriguing sense of humour. After a pause, she checked my father's drug chart before turning her attention back to me.

"I will leave you two in peace, but I am sure I will see you again."

"Probably tomorrow?" I said, trying not to gaze at her too long.

"Yes, you will definitely see me tomorrow. Be good now, you," she said with a smile, giving Dad a gentle tap on the shoulder.

"See you tomorrow." I watched her exit the room, feeling myself missing her presence immediately, but I wasn't there to ogle a nurse. I was there for my father and needed to focus on that. Once we were alone, I moved myself closer to Dad. Mentally absent, he continued to stare at the ceiling. I grabbed his hand, cool to the touch, squeezing it gently, to make my presence known. "Dad, I have to go back to work soon, back to Edinburgh."

He said nothing, keeping his vision firmly fixed to the ceiling above.

I talked, pausing periodically as if to give him a chance to speak. He never did, but occasionally would tilt his head in my direction. I became emotional, longing for some sign of connection that was noticeably absent that day.

"Do you know I am here? Dad, can you hear me?"

Silence.

"I hope you do wherever you are, you know I am here. Guess I'll never know."

I sat with him for an hour in silence. Occasionally, he would say words which made no sense to me, even if it would initially spark a sense of hope. The bed seemed to dwarf him. I hated myself for not getting there sooner. I hated myself for staying away for so long. For a long time, the only movement I saw was the laboured rise and fall of his chest.

Just as I was about to leave, Ainsley popped back in, and judging by her startled response, she was unaware I was still there. "I am so sorry," she said, alarmed, oblivious to my presence disguised in the faint bedside shadow.

"It's okay. I am going now. It's getting late," I mumbled as I brought myself to a stand.

"Did you get anything out of him?" she queried, walking around to the left side of his bed to tuck him in again as he somehow evaded his covers in his erratic movements.

"Not today, no. Will I? Will I ever get anything back?"

She paused as if to digest my question. "Finn, it is such an individual thing it's hard to say."

"I can see why they suggested counselling then," I mumbled.

"Who suggested that?"

"Dr Wells did."

She nodded, smoothing the top blanket over Dad's legs. "I guess it doesn't do any harm. When I lost my mother, I found it difficult to connect with someone who had no experience of it themselves. It can be useful."

"I don't enjoy talking about it to anyone. I'm sorry you lost your mother."

"Do you have much support? Wife? Friends? Family?" Her rapid glance at me before she turned back to dad made me wonder if she was searching for more insight into me. "It's fine. It happened years ago now. Feels like yesterday, though. Funny thing, life is, you realise around here how fast it really goes."

"I can relate to that. My mother died earlier this year, but sometimes it feels like it was just yesterday." With any other woman who asked, I wouldn't feel inclined to answer, but with Ainsley, I wanted to. "I'm not married, and my friends are all busy in their own lives. Plus, it all feels quite morbid, you know? How am I meant to tell people how I feel when I don't even know myself? I just know, it's hard to see him like this."

"Maybe counselling might help, then?" she replied, carefully unbuttoning a row of shoulder buttons on my father's gown. "It is hard. Nobody tells you how hard it is. It's not a linear grief."

"I'm sorry. I shouldn't be saying all of this." I said apologetically, realising how much I divulged.

"It comes with the job, don't apologise."

"You already deal with all of this; you do not need your patient's family giving you all their unresolved emotional baggage too."

She let out a laugh, running a series of chords through the open slit in my dad's gown to connect him to the heart rate monitor.

"Well, I don't get paid enough for that, but I don't mind. Finn, I am happy to listen if it helps you get through. It's nice to help people, especially when I have been in the position you are."

"Thank you. I can see why your patients like you." I watched as she pressed several buttons on the monitor, and it sprang to life, filling the room with its periodic beeps.

She said nothing as she walked over to the washbasin to wash her hands, observing herself in the mirror with two brief glances.

"Can I make one suggestion, Finn?"

"Of course."

"Don't be hard on yourself. If there is anything, anything I have learnt is that this road, which I am sure you have guessed by now, comes with a whole raft of emotions. I used to not understand why some people would just drop their partner, mother, father, sister, brother off here and walk away. I now realise in my ignorance not everyone can deal with the emotions that come with this journey. It isn't easy. Take a lot of empathy for yourself and the situation at hand."

"I will try," I replied as I walked towards the door.

"Have a good evening."

"You too. See you tomorrow, Dad."

The 7 Stages of Grief

That evening, I lay in bed unable to sleep, reflecting on Ainsley's comment on how grief wasn't linear. I never heard someone use that term before and yet, it felt so fitting. My experience after my mother passed was definitely not a straight line and even years later, I had days where I couldn't escape the guilt.

I never told my mother about my diagnosis of PTSD, but I think she eventually put two and two together. One weekend I went home, and she came across my half-used bottle of Sertraline.

Given her nursing background, my mother knew exactly what the prescription was. That afternoon, while Roger and Dad tinkered in the shed, I knew she had questions when she sat me down at the dining room table

"Do you want to talk about it?" she questioned; her blue eyes fixed on me.

"Not really," I said quietly, doing my best to avert my gaze.

She paused, taking a sip of her tea.

"Why didn't you tell me, Finn? Is this where you have been? You know I would have understood. We could have helped you."

I knew she meant well and would have done her best to understand. I didn't doubt that for a second. She would never have been able to understand completely as she had not experienced what I had. I shrugged, unsure of how to answer her.

"I'm worried about you." she said, keeping her eyes firmly fixed on me.

"You don't need to be." I tried not to sound dismissive.

I could tell she didn't believe me in the slightest by her frown. My mother always had such an expressive face, and it was never hard to establish what she was thinking.

"I'm fine. Seriously, Ma, don't worry."

She took another sip of her tea, running her finger around the lip of the mug. "You will come to know one day, Finn, when you have children of your own, that it isn't something you can switch off."

She never directly questioned me about it again but dropped subtle questions from that day on in our phone calls. Vague questions if I had gone out drinking and if I still attended my appointments.

Towards the end of her journey, nothing helped me evade the grief of my year long absence. When I eventually came right, my mother was not who I remembered. The cancer weakened her, and I think the prospect of death changed her outlook on life. Even though she never dwelled on it, it was as if the day she found out there was no exit from her journey; she lost the thirst she once had for life. In ways others wouldn't understand, she tried to find that hunger. Pushing herself physically to her limits, climbing mountains and training for a marathon she never got to complete. As much as she tried, what was lost could never be regained.

Towards the end of my deployment, I was in a dire contact and it was one of the very few occasions I needed her; really needed her. When I eventually got the chance to call her two days later, she was vomiting from her chemotherapy, struggling to hold our very brief conversation. When my PTSD made itself known, the memory of that very conversation ultimately put the final nail in my decision to separate myself until I felt I wouldn't burden her when she was already evidently struggling.

I expected to experience grief naturally from her passing but what I didn't realise is what that would look like.

Six months before my mother passed after the initial period of disbelief and shock had waned, I found myself in a well of grief I never saw coming.

The guilt intoxicated me. I fixated on missed opportunities caused by my absence and questioned if I hadn't gone on deployment, maybe I would have noticed she was sick before it was too late. To numb the feelings, I turned to alcohol, which thrust me back into the arms of PTSD again. After not having a nightmare for months, I started to have horrific night terrors again. I started not eating and not functioning properly, angry and ashamed. I became better at hiding it, able to keep it under the radar. Unlike before, I wasn't able to hide away and wait for it to pass because without my mother, my father was alone and his health showed clear signs it was fast deteriorating. I did my best at coping, but as I reflected, I realised I wasn't coping; I was surviving.

My father noticed something was amiss one evening when he observed me drinking. It had been a bad day, triggered when my father decided he was ready to donate several items of my mother's clothing she could no longer wear. My mother was in the hospital at the time after getting a pneumonia infection, which caused her to become unwell very quickly. I convinced myself that was it, and with that, I became furious.

"Finn, I think you have had enough," he said in a quiet, yet stern, voice as I reached for another drink.

I looked over at him, seated in his chair as he stared back at me. I was on a fine line between intoxicated and not and for reasons that evade me, I became angry with him.

"Excuse me?" I questioned, placing my unopened beer down next to me.

"I said I think you have had enough."

There was a moment of silence where I looked at him angered with him staring at me back with a blank, unphased expression.

"Coming from you," I retorted, reaching for my bottle.

"As your father, I think you have had enough. Since when did you drink, Finn? You have never been a drinker."

I paused; my fingers wrapped around the neck of the bottle before the words fell out of my mouth. "What would you know? You have no fucking idea who I am, Da. You spent half of my life out at fucking sea. We don't talk. You don't know who I am so let's get one thing straight, don't act like you fucking know me when you don't."

While my father spent a lot of time at sea, when he was home, he had been nothing but a good father, even if I struggled to understand him. Unlike my mother, he seldom showed much emotion. Hugs and kisses were a rarity for me growing up, and when they happened, they often struck me as lifeless, something he did because he felt he was supposed to, not because he wanted to. My mother said it was a cultural thing as my grandfather was very much the same, but it would be a lie to say there weren't times when I struggled with it. I know he loved me in his own way but struggled with the comparison of affections he gave to my mother.

The air became very tense, and he froze, unsure of what to say.

"Are you going to say anything?" I demanded as I stared at him.

He looked to his feet and took a deep inhalation of breath. I knew whatever he was about to say would be non-confrontational as it wasn't in his personality to be anything but.

"Do you remember when we went to Edinburgh, and we went and saw the castles?" he started. "You were always so fascinated with history."

I shook my head, all the frustration of life with my dad coming to the surface. "What are you trying to say?" I shouted at him. "You think you know me because we spent a handful of occasions together throughout my childhood because you were always at fucking sea. You hear me? You were always at fucking sea, Da."

He said nothing, but I'll never forget his pained expression when he stood silently and made his way up-stairs. I'd hurt him, and though I told myself I hadn't wanted to, deep down I think a part of me did.

The following morning, after a night of restless sleep, I heard my father crying in his bedroom. I stood outside his door, peering through the small gap and watched. He sat bent over the end of the bed, clutching a photograph of my mother, his body thinning and hair ruffled.

"Da," I said, with a gentle knock on the door.

He glanced in my direction, not saying a word.

"Can I come in?"

He nodded, and I took a seat next to him on the bed.

"I'm sorry. I didn't mean any of it." I said after a moment of silence.

"I don't want her to go." He placed the picture face down next to him on the bed. "I was wrong to tell you what to do. You are a grown man after all."

I shook my head with a heaved sigh. "Da, I feel guilty. Guilty I wasn't here. I'm so angry with myself. She deserved better."

"Did she ever teach you about the seven stages of grief?" He sidestepped my admission, changing the subject. "She wanted me to understand so I could recognise it in both of us when the end comes. Knowing that you and I are as stubborn as each other."

"The seven stages of grief?" I questioned, studying his face.

He looked down at the floor, his eyes watery. "She told me, clinically, there are seven stages of grief. She..." He laughed as he gave me a slight smile. "She told me that when the anger comes, not to take it personally."

"Well, that is something." I laughed. Of course. My mother, always one step ahead, would have said that.

"She bought me a book," he said as he brought himself to a stand and walked over to the bookcase. He studied the colourful row of hardcovers for a moment before he pulled the third one from the right out and handed it to me. "She made me read this."

I look down at the cover with the words *The Seven Stages of Grieving* in bold text. "Did you read it?"

He paused, giving me a smirk. "Some of it."

"Some of it?"

"The bits I think I needed to read."

That evening, I flicked through the book and came across the chapter titled *Guilt*. Word for word, it all seemed to make sense even if some of the text felt very generic and contrived, nothing felt out of place. I could see myself on those pages; my own emotions being described by a perfect stranger.

I hadn't picked up the book since that day, but as I lie, unable to sleep, something was pulling me to read it again. One of the most difficult things while watching my father's demise was feeling grief but not in the context of normal loss. The grief was sustained, a slow and painful process watching my father lose all that I had once known, yet still seeing his face every day. The hopes that swelled on a good day to only be abruptly ripped from under me the next. Not knowing how it would end or when and whether he would remember who I was on his last day.

I made my way downstairs to grab it from the bookshelf, flooded with a sense of déjà vu. As I took a seat on the couch, lit by the soft glow of the streetlights, I opened the first page.

Each word my eyes read told me what I already knew. I had been there before.

Good Days, Bad Days

The following morning, I went for a run to prepare for my return to work. I hadn't been consistent about it since my return home. After a quick shower and a bite to eat, I felt ready to face the day, knowing I wouldn't see Dad till the following weekend. I dreaded going back to Edinburgh, but the bills were mounting faster than I expected.

When I arrived, he was in the downstairs common area again, sitting with Ainsley and another nurse as they tried to coax him into eating some food.

"Not eating?" I pulled a seat from the table next to his to sit down.

"Unfortunately, we are not having a good day," Ainsley said, keeping her focus on him.

"Seems to be having a lot of those lately," I muttered under my breath.

The other nurse, one whom I did not recognise, looked down at her watch before she gently tapped Ainsley on the forearm. "I have to do the rounds and I will come back," she said quietly before excusing herself from the table.

Ainsley kept trying with her best efforts to make the food appetising to Dad when my thoughts were interrupted by a well-dressed gentleman as he sat down next to a woman seated three tables over. The woman looked frail, dressed in a long-sleeved, peach coloured dress shirt and beige capris. As she stared into space, she looked visibly lost in her own world, occasionally muttering to herself.

"Hello beautiful, how are you?" he asked as he pulled a seat beside her.

The lady appeared a little flustered and confused, unable to recognise the gentleman before her.

"I'm fine, thank you. How has your day been?" she said, staring at him with her eyebrows drawn together.

"Well, my dear, my day is much better now that I have seen you. Daniel gave me this haircut. Do you like it?" he asked. He smiled at her, smoothing his hand over balding, thin hair, trimmed at the sides.

"Daniel?" she questioned as the parallel lines between her brows deepened, and she tilted her head to the side.

Her confusion clearly didn't bother the man as he laid a single red rose across the table. "Daniel is our son, dear. He picked this for you from your garden. It smells divine. You always loved the red ones."

Paying no attention to the rose, the woman scowled. "A son? We have a son?"

"Yes, my dear. We have a son. A daughter, too. We are married and have had the most beautiful of lives. We didn't get the beach house we wanted, but, my dear, we are here together and that is all that matters for me. I must go now, eat your breakfast and be kind to the nurses, would you? I will be back later." He brought himself to a stand, taking a moment to look at her. "I will be back, my love," he said before he disappeared out of view. A short time later, the nurse that had been seated with Ainsley when I arrived walked over to her to query where he had gone.

"Beats me," the woman said with a shrug. "I think I'll get a haircut at the beach. Who was he anyway?"

"True love, that is." Ainsley said as she studied the woman left sitting on her own.

"He comes here every day with a rose and then he comes back after a while and just watches her from afar. It is one thing you see in this place. How love, in its rarest forms, is so beautiful."

Dad, who said nothing since my arrival, murmured something as he took a sip of his tea.

I barely heard Dad talk for over a week and formed the realisation that I may never hear his voice again.

"Is this all I am going to get from now?" I questioned, changing the subject, reaching for my father's hand, which felt bone-like and lukewarm under my grip.

"Hard to say, Finn. Sometimes they come back to us in fleeting moments."

"Has he talked much this week?"

She let out a laugh, as if she found my question oddly humorous. "He gave me quite the story that you were a naughty teenager, I think maybe two days ago?"

"I really was not that bad."

"Oh, he thinks you were. Always sneaking out of the house to see girls, apparently."

"Oh really?" I glanced at her with my eyebrows raised.

"Apparently so. Pinching his whisky too, I hear."

"That happened once," I said, grinning.

"I know this may come across as strange, but, Finn, I love his stories about you and your mother. I've met a lot of people in this job, some who have had unfortunate family lives, and when they are always so bitter about their pasts. Your father, well, whenever he is lost in his world, I can only tell you he is always smiling."

I looked at Dad, feeling emotion brewing from Ainsley's words. She saw parts of him that were coming fewer and far between for me and it brought me comfort to know that at least in the moments he was present, he was happy.

"I'm sorry," I said as I let out a sniff, nervously looking at the floor.

"Why are you sorry?" she laughed. "Don't be daft."

"I find myself asking how long I have. He talks to you, but I feel I'm never going to hear any form of proper words come out of his mouth again."

"He might surprise you. They often do."

"Aye, you're right he might, but I have to go back to work for two weeks. I don't know whether he is going to be alive in two weeks for me to come back to."

She looked at me for a moment, not saying a word.

"This is very unethical, but I need to ask you something."

"Go on," I said, intrigued. I sensed whatever was coming wasn't good, given her hesitancy.

"Do you want my honest opinion, or do you want me to tell you what you want to hear?"

I looked at her, startled as she kept a sincere but serious face. "Well, obviously I want you to be honest?"

"Good, because sometimes you never know. Look, I could tell you to leave and go back to work and he will be exactly the same in two weeks' time, but if you want my honest opinion, I don't think you have long. Finn, I hate telling people this, and I don't always get it right, but I sense with your dad here he is ready to go. He is just waiting for the body to do the same."

"I appreciate your honesty," I said, my vision blurred from the tears I forcibly tried to hold back.

"I never enjoy lying to people and Finn, I could be wrong. I-." She paused mid thought as if to assess what she was about to say. "Finn, I got it wrong with my mother. I lost time. Time I can never get back. I know a lot of people think work and all these other things are important, but, well, once they are gone, they are gone. If you want my advice, I would take the next week or two off work. Personally, if it was me, I would spend as much time as possible with him as he is or not. It may feel insignificant to him, but in the long term it will be hugely significant to you."

"Wait, your own mother?" I questioned, looking at her, confused, wondering if I misheard her.

She held my gaze for a moment, piercing me with her green eyes before she began writing on her notepad.

"Yes, my mother had this awful disease, too. The

difference is, well, she escaped the house one day, and I never saw her alive again." She stopped writing for a second, glancing up as if to gauge my reaction from my silence. "Sorry I am sometimes too open."

"No, no," I replied, shaking my head. "I... I appreciate this. I just... I... I don't know what to say. That is, well, horrific."

"It is, but it is also more common than people think. My problem was, my mother was very, very smart. She fooled one of the in-home carers into believing she was having a sleep in one morning when I was at work. In reality, in her mind, she plotted her escape. She spent the night out in the middle of the winter in Swords, dressed in nothing but her nightie. Unfortunately, she could never survive those conditions."

I sat numbed, unsure how to respond.

"Ainsley, I'm sorry... That is..."

She smiled, checking her watch on her left wrist. "No need to be sorry, Finn, it's life, and it is why I am doing this job. At least you know your dad is in safe hands."

She glanced in my direction; her lips pursed.

"Finn, I mean this in a truly, genuine and heartfelt way. I am always happy to listen if you need it. I really struggled with the whole counselling side of things. It is something I am sure you will get encouraged to partake in, but I personally didn't find it that useful for me. Sometimes it is nice to have someone to listen to who has been there themselves, so anytime if you ever need help, call me."

She scribbled down her number on one of the back pages of her notepad before tearing it off.

"Do you do this for all your patients?" I jokingly questioned as she slid the piece of paper across the table in my direction.

"Well, no," she said, flustered. "But I have a soft spot for your dad. He really is quite funny."

"Must be where I get it from," I replied, smirking as I stuck the piece of paper into my pocket.

"Think about what I said regarding taking some time off. I could be wrong, Finn. I just... I sense it and would feel I have an obligation to tell you."

I appreciated her honesty, even if it was hard to digest. I knew I was going to lose him, but the realisation was hard that the months I thought I had left were becoming weeks, and fast approaching days.

"I sense it too. I guess I didn't want to admit it."

She nodded in agreement, studying Dad's face.

"I suppose I best get work organised."

"I think that is a decision you won't regret, Finn. I mean it."

One of the kitchen orderlies came over and took away Dad's uneaten plates. Ainsley brought herself to a stand.

"You can take him out any time. I'm sure he would enjoy that. Wouldn't you?" She smiled, tapping his shoulder lightly with no response. "You will just need to take a chair, but we can organise one of those."

As I stood, realising visiting time was over, I glanced briefly over at the far-right corner of the common area where I could see the man from earlier sitting and watching the woman from afar.

His face expressed the epitome of devotion as he lovingly stared at the woman, who no longer remembered who he was. Of all the lessons I took away from seeing Dad that Sunday morning, the realisation that I had a choice hit me the hardest. I had lost track of all the positive memories I once held with my father. They became blended and misplaced with the new memories that were forming in his illness because of my resentment. The identity of who he was, who we were as father and son, ended up distorted as I desperately tried to hold on to the man I once knew.

The man, as he watched his wife, knew she didn't know he was there. But he chose to not allow the disease to affect his memories of her. Evident from his actions, full of love, their life had once existed with such passion.

I knew then I had a choice over the coming weeks, knowing his life was fast approaching his end. I could choose to embrace his disease instead of trying to fight it and resent it and know that even though he was not here with me, the memories still were.

White Roses

When I visited my father the following morning, he said nothing for the first fifteen minutes. I stared at him, watching as he focused out the window, wondering if perhaps on this day he didn't recognise me. Days like this were becoming frequent, and I felt remorseful about showing up this way. When I showed up without warning, I found myself burdened with questions if it was becoming too hard on him. Finally, he took a deep breath and smiled.

"Hello, Finn. It's good to see you." His voice was weak and raspy, but I found relief in the knowledge I had him back for a fleeting visit.

I slowly smiled with an amazement in my eyes. "How are you today, Da?"

He brought his hand to his chin, rubbing the sparse stubble. "I had eggs for breakfast."

"You always liked your eggs," I replied, wheeling his wheelchair to the right of the bed.

I originally wanted to take my father out into the country, but one of his appointments to check his kidneys had been changed at the last minute, so I decided just to spend time with him on the grounds.

Part of my choice in selecting the right care home for him was that it needed to have a garden. Not just an ordinary garden, I knew it would need to have one where my father could get lost in his world, comforted by pockets of colour. In his later years, my father was a keen gardener with a fascination for bees, planting all he could to attract them, just so he could watch them. No longer physically able to find solace in the sea, he seemed to find a sense of regularity and structure tending to his garden instead.

The April sky was clear as we made our way out into the garden. The temperature hovered in the mid-teens, with just enough breeze to carry the perfumed aroma of flowers.

"The tulips will be gone soon. Shame that. She always liked the tulips," he said, leaning forward slightly in his chair as I parked him next to a bunch of ageing tulips.

"Who did?"

He smiled, keeping his focus away from my own. "Your mother."

I stiffened, unsure if it was a sign I was losing him. I longed for one day where we could just talk as we used to. "She loved white roses too, didn't she?"

"Aye, yes she did, but tulips, no, those were her favourite."

There was a pause in his words before he laughed, shaking his head lightly in recollection of a memory. "When we first dated, I would always pinch her flowers from an elderly woman's garden a block or two from her house."

I smiled, seeing the joy written on his face as he relayed the story to me.

"The house was derelict, but the garden was astonishing. I think the woman lived alone. Kids would always joke that she escaped the asylum, but I think she was just lonely."

I smiled as I studied his face. His mouth creased at the corners of his wide, enthusiastic grin.

"She also loved these Belgium chocolates from the confectionery store. They were expensive, Finny. I was only making a couple of shillings a week from the lumberyard and would spend a fortnight's wages just to buy her a box of twelve."

Before joining the navy, my father worked part time in a lumberyard at the docks. He lied about his age, working there from a mere twelve years of age when they thought he was actually sixteen.

"Ye really loved her, didn't ye, Da?" I said to him, giving his hand a gentle squeeze.

"Aye Finny, I did."

"I never asked ye, Da. How did ya meet?"

It was a lie, but I could see how much talking about her was making him happy. My father met my mother when they were both fourteen. My mother was a gifted artist and had the career not been shunned by her highly academic parents, it was rightly something she could have sustained herself financially doing. One day she watched my father playing with his childhood dog, a white highland terrier called Jack, drawing him from afar. All it took was a wayward ball to land in her lap, and the rest was history.

My mother's parents never agreed to the match between them both. Given my father had grown up just above the poverty line, the societal views of them both caused a lot of disparity. I had little to do with my grandparents because of it. Agnes always maintained they would get over it, but they never did. When my grandparents both passed within weeks of each other shortly after her diagnosis, she realised just how much their disapproval ran when they donated their estate to charity. She was never bitter about it, but it evidently upset her. How could it not?

As my father relayed the story to me, right down to the yellow frock she was wearing, I couldn't help but smile. He always worried he would forget her, but part of me believed in his lucid moments he never fully would.

We sat in silence for a moment, our ears tuned to a lone honeybee making its way between the flowers.

When he piped up again, I sensed his mind was slipping. As he continued to relay stories of their youthful dates, he would occasionally call me William. His words became jumbled, and he would throw me periodic confused glares as if to try to re-figure who I was. His words became too rapid. It was hard to establish in the end what he was trying to say. I knew that most days he just needed me to listen, but when he lost himself, I found it hard, questioning if he even knew who I was.

"There you two are," Ainsley interrupted, walking towards us with her cheeks flushed. "I have been looking for you everywhere."

"Sorry, I thought I would get him some fresh air," I replied as I stood to greet her.

"No need to be sorry for that. Sounds like a perfectly

reasonable idea. I just needed to get him ready for his appointment and did not know where he was!"

I glanced at my watch, realising the hour I thought we had been outside was actually nearing three.

"Sorry, I must have lost track of time."

"I'm sure he would have loved it."

We made our way back inside, my father now deep in his own world again.

"What did you guys talk about?" Ainsley questioned as we entered the elevator.

"Flowers."

"Flowers?"

I laughed. "Aye, flowers and my mother."

Ainsley nodded, swiping her key card to mobilise the elevator. "He has been talking a lot about her lately."

"I think he knows."

"Knows?" she questioned in reply, fixing her name tag on a heavy lean.

"That he is going to be with her soon."

"What are you doing this afternoon?" Ainsley questioned in an effort to change the subject; a look of uncomfortableness spread over her face.

"I am going to go visit my friend Blair. You met him a few weeks ago."

"The other red head?" She said with a laugh.

"Aye, that one."

She nodded, but there was something enchanting about her demeanour. As I watched her bend down to check on my father, lips slightly parted, I felt an almost hypnotic pull. She must have sensed it too, for when her gaze drifted from my father to meet mine, she hastily retreated her gaze before she came to a stand.

"Well, I hope you have fun," she said with a hint of unease in her voice.

Normally, I wouldn't have thought twice about it, but as I made my way to meet Blair at the bar, I seemed unable to shake it. The Brig was always somewhere we had gone growing up for one of their infamous hand battered haggis fritters and fries.

We made our way over to our usual table in the far-right corner, taking a seat.

"How is the nurse?" Blair questioned as he panned the bar.

"Fine," I replied with reluctance, sensing his intrigue.

"Fine? Is that all?"

I stared at him for a moment with a sarcastic smile. "It's not happening."

"If you say so."

I could tell from the sardonic tones in his voice there wasn't an ounce of belief in my words.

The barmaid arrived with our pints and a bowl of hot chips generously up sized.

"This place is legendary for its hospitality," I said as we both thanked her.

"How's ye da?" Blair asked, reaching for a chip. "Are ye doing okay?"

"He is doing okay, just hard. We will get there though."

"I don't know what to say, Finny. Is there anything I can do?"

"Nay, we're right," I replied as I took a sip of my pint.

Blair was deep in thought, staring into the distance in a trance. "Finny, I ain't too good at the moment," he eventually said. "Things have been coming back to me."

"From Afghanistan?"

"Aye."

"What things?"

Blair paused as he ran his finger over the lip of his glass. "Just everything. The Black Friday, everything."

I knew the contact he meant as it was one that plagued me for several months upon my return. "You need to see someone."

"I don't talk, Finny. I'm good, I'll get through it. Shell knows; she has been a good help."

A lot of my PTSD revolved around the contact those of us involved called our Black Friday. For months after I returned, whenever I glanced in the mirror, I was reminded of what happened that day. We had been involved in a contact when our lead vehicle on a routine patrol to an outpost was struck by an IED. After the explosion, we came under quite heavy small arms fire, and we ended up losing three comrades in the contact, one of which was

Ed. Blair, Ed and I joined at the same time and, combined with Colin, we became a pack of four. One was never far without the others. For me, I battled with the ghost of not being able to save Ed. For months, I seemed unable to move past it. His wounds were non-survivable from the blast, but at the height of my PTSD, I fixated on all I could have done differently. Blair lost half of his right ear. A human head doesn't look quite natural with half an ear, but eventually he became accustomed to it. While my scars were now buried, for Blair, he faced the reality of it every day. Try wearing sunglasses with just one functional ear and you'll understand why.

"Don't do that," I said to him as I tried to catch his gaze.

"Do what?"

"Don't dismiss it."

"I'm not," he said with a shrug, leaning back in his chair.

"It will get to you."

"Only if I let it," he replied with a grin. It was no laughing matter given I know how much it affected me, but it wasn't my right to invade how he wanted to tackle it. I took a sip of my pint in silence, unsure how to respond.

"I think my da is getting sick too, Finny. Ma blames the fags."

"Sick how?"

"His lungs ain't too good."

"Has he been to see anyone?" I questioned.

Blair shook his head. "Refuses to. Stubborn he is."

"What does ye ma think?"

"She is trying, Finny, but he's hard work. Ye know that."

I nodded, knowing full well what Blair's father was like. "The stubbornness will kill him."

"Try telling him that, Finny. Like talking to a brick wall."

"What are you going to do?"

"Not much we can do. Keep trying, I guess," Blair countered with a shrug.

That evening I couldn't help but lay awake in reflection of Blair's words. Even though I made gains in how I handled my emotions surrounding what happened over there, knowing he was battling brought it back into my own headlights. When I found myself in my reflection, I realised how lonely I was even when I wouldn't admit it. Over the course of the evening, Blair told me Michelle and him would navigate it and he would be okay, and the stark realisation hit me. I had nobody. My father was my only close family left, and we hadn't had a proper conversation in what felt like forever. I buried my head into my pillow, a stem of emotion brewing within my layers. For what felt like the hundredth time that month, I cried, knowing life was changing and I simply could not keep up.

The Little Boy Who Said Nil

Blair, for as long as I had known him, was always vocal about his emotions. He revealed himself so freely. For me, the very concept was quite the contrary. Since I was a child, I had always been an observer, one to never say much. It copped my fair chunk of bullying as a child, as I was always the quiet one, yet when I needed to be I could be quite the little 'runt' as Blair's father would call me.

It wasn't until I joined the army that I was forced to change my ways. I would have rather spent my nights reading Stephen King novels and playing guitar than at the bar, but that wasn't the culture I fell into when I joined. Slowly I read less and the more nights I spent out, the less socially awkward I became.

It wasn't until I started treatment for my PTSD; I realised no matter how much I changed, part of me would always be that little boy.

The little boy who said very little.

Dr Kent often queried what I was like as a child. Nodding when I relayed to him, I was the quiet, studious, yet aggressive underdog in our group. He remarked it made perfect sense how I was. I didn't understand what he meant by that and still don't, though I guessed it might have been linked to the way I internalised emotions.

I reluctantly organised to meet with one counsellor through the organisation, Dr Wells suggested, holding onto the faintest hope they would help me understand my emotions. I had become increasingly angry about the situation. I expected anger, but not to the degree I was. I dreaded my visits, unsure if I could emotionally cope with who would present themselves on the day.

I arrived at the office two blocks from the care facility shortly after ten that morning and was greeted by a middle-aged brunette woman saturated in perfume.

"Good morning, Finn. It is lovely to meet you," she said, extending her hand. "I am Dr Grant. Come with me. My office is down the corridor."

I followed her down the dimly lit corridor, taking the second to last door before a pair of fire exit doors. "Take a seat."

I sat down in a bright red leathered tube seat, unsure of where to look. I scanned the walls, looking for something to fixate on that would take me away from the situation I found myself in. Just like all the offices, the walls were coated in distracting imagery, but instead of brains and wild animals, there were many paintings and photos of different countries.

"So, Finn, tell me how I can help? I have briefly reached out with Dr Wells. He mentioned your father has quite progressive dementia. Is that correct?"

"That is correct," I replied quietly.

"That must be hard. It is such an awful disease."

I shrugged, feeling nervous. "Yes,"

"How does it make you feel?"

I paused, staring directly at her for a moment.

"Well, I'm angry."

"That is understandable," she replied, taking a sip of water. "I see a lot of patients come through these doors that feel the same. How are you coping with that anger?"

If I was coping with my anger, I wouldn't be here, I thought to myself, dubious of how to reply.

"I'm sensing that coping might be the issue," she said as she glanced down at her hands. "What I am trying to establish here, Finn, is how I can best help you. You haven't given me much to go off."

I glared at her with a creased brow. Ainsley was right. How did I expect her to understand?

"This was a waste of time," I muttered, bringing myself to a stand.

"If you like, I can get one of the other doctors and see if they are free," she said anxiously.

"No," I replied as I shook my head before making my way to the door. "I will sort this myself."

Back in the safety of my car, I slammed my hands against the dash, which caused a wave of pain to radiate through my knuckles. I didn't understand why I was so angry. During my PTSD treatments, Dr Wells asked me whether I found shame in discussing my emotions. Whilst this was partially factual, it wasn't the sole foundation as to why I felt a need not to discuss my inner workings with people. I didn't see it as problematic, but I think others did.

I took a deep breath, sinking myself into the blue cloth seats. Ainsley was right, I thought again to myself as I reached for my phone. I still had her number tucked into the back pocket of my jeans, and I felt compelled to tell her about the disastrous attempt at a counselling session.

That was a disaster

Finn

I placed my phone down on the warm dashboard, illuminated by the midmorning sun. I wasn't sure if Ainsley was at work yet or not, but to my surprise, two minutes later, my phone vibrated.

I'm sorry to hear that. It isn't for everyone.

Are you okay?

Ainsley

I stared down at my phone screen as I pondered her question. Despite my anger, I knew I would be okay even if I momentarily wasn't.

I'm fine. I just thought I would share a pointless piece of information. Are you not at work?

Finn

I glanced up at a couple walking past, immersed in deep conversation. They looked to be in their mid-sixties, throwing their heads back in laughter. I smiled and my thoughts wandered to how my mother and father used to be. The way he spoke about her yesterday, in how he remembered the most minute of details about their start in this life. The ways his eyes lit up as he spoke about her, even after all this time. Perhaps that afternoon I would bring some pictures of her with me, I thought to myself.

No, I am not on till 2pm. May or may not see you then.

Ainsley

I paused, wondering how to reply to her message without seeming flirtatious. In the end, I didn't reply and made the journey back to my father's to find some more clothing for him. He had become frailer with each passing day and I knew it would only be a matter of time before I would have to buy him new clothing, but I wasn't ready to do that yet. Oddly, sometimes just seeing an old piece of clothing triggered memories of him I didn't even know were there.

Last week, I dug out from the bottom of his wardrobe an old, faded Sex Pistols t-shirt. I never knew my father liked the band and yet underneath the shirt were more punk rock items. A pair of old ripped knee jeans and boots I couldn't even imagine my father wearing, yet that afternoon when I showed him, his face lit up in a way I had never seen before.

"I remember those things," he said with a wide grin, his eyes twinkling.

I placed the shirt on his lap and the boots at the foot of the bed. I was eager to know the story behind the attire if he could remember and remember, he did.

Though his voice had become strained, he did his best to tell me about a concert he and my mother attended in the late seventies. Just like in the garden the day before, I was amazed by the small details he could remember. Dr Wells warned me the long-term memory tended to be the last to go, but seeing it was something else. In some ways, it was comforting. If he couldn't live in the present, at least for now, he could live happily in the past, even if I will never know the factual accuracy of those memories.

Dr Wells also briefly touched on the fact my father would most likely revert to his past emotive memories. Memories that triggered emotions in him, which I found to be accurate, as he often referred to times with my mother. While it saddened me that the memories of my childhood were fading, getting to know the parts of him when I wasn't alive had its joyous moments, too.

"I remember when they started. We were three back from the front," he said in a murmur, running his hands over the cracked paint imagery on the shirt. "I had only just come back from sea and promised your mother I would take her."

I smiled. "Did you guys have fun?"

"We had more than fun, Finny. Had to be one of the best concerts I ever went to."

"I didn't know you liked that music."

"I was a big fan of The Who, Deep Purple, and Led Zeppelin," he mused.

"No." I said with a grin. For as long as I had known him, my father had listened to old folk music artists such as Dougie MacLean and Archie Fisher.

"Ooh yes, your mother loved the more punk styled music, but I much preferred my rock."

"Well, I have learnt something," I whispered, watching as his eyes became startled. "You all right, Da?"

He ignored the question as he pushed the shirt off him to the floor. He had lost his bearings on where he was and did his best to scan the room in a frenzied panic.

"Da, it's okay," I said as I gently placed my hand on his forearm.

"I'm sorry I... I don't know where I am."

"It's okay, it's okay. You are in your bed with me, Finn. I am your son."

"My son?"

"Aye, that's right." I replied, as I did my best to re-assure him.

"No, you are mistaken."

He tried to distance himself from me to reach up and press the call button from behind his bed.

"Da, please."

"No, no, no." He shook his head, his voice trembling as he muttered no repeatedly.

"Everything okay here?" I heard Ainsley from behind me as she walked around to the right of my father's bed. "

"Got ourselves a wee bit confused, have we?" she said with a smile as she brought herself to his eye level. "Hello you."

"Do I..."

"Aye, yes you do. I am Ainsley, and that young gentle-man is your son, Finn."

He glanced over at me, his eyes wide. "Where am I?"

"You are home. You live here now, and I take care of you. You're not the only one. You have friends who also get confused. Jenny, from two down? She forgot where she was today too."

I watched her as she effortlessly seemed to calm him and he relaxed, becoming one with his bed again as she tucked him in.

"How did you do that?" I questioned once she turned her attention back to me.

"Do what?"

"Seem so... I don't know. Calm?"

"Practice and patience."

"Well, clearly I have neither."

She stared at me with compassion in her eyes. "Early days."

"He is forgetting me, but somehow he can remember a concert that happened half a lifetime ago."

I didn't mean to sound angry, but she sensed the anger in my words, averting her gaze to my father's drug chart. "What happened this morning?" she questioned, as she checked the time.

"Well, she wanted me to explain why I was angry."

Ainsley let out an uncontrolled laugh. "And you are meant to explain that how?"

"That is what I thought too."

"Will you try someone else?"

"Well, if today is anything to go off, absolutely not."

"They aren't all like that," Ainsley said with a brief glance over her shoulder in my direction.

"Well, to be honest with you, I don't think I want to

even try."

"That might change. Where do you think you will go tomorrow?" she questioned, shifting the subject.

"I thought we might try to go fishing or something. Maybe just go for a drive."

"That sounds like a nice idea."

There was a moment's silence as I could see she had more to say but pondered how best to say it out loud.

"Finn," she finally said, her voice hesitant.

"Yes?"

"Just be careful. I know you are doing all you can trying to use this time, but it is best not to have expectations because one thing I have learnt is that it's a sure-fire way to disappoint yourself. I know it sounds contradictory-."

"It doesn't," I replied, cutting her off. "I know what you mean."

She smiled, giving me a brief nod. "Have a good evening."

"You too."

Hope

That next day I took Dad out to Aberdeenshire, forty minutes from the city to visit a loch he had taken me to shortly after my twelfth birthday.

Mum's sister Agnes brought a fishing rod for my birthday with the promise the first fish I caught was hers. I had never been fishing, and it was something Dad seemed to have actively avoided whenever it was suggested. I would come to learn it wasn't because he didn't want to, he simply didn't know how.

Despite spending most of his life at sea, Dad never mastered the art of fishing and after weeks of my persistent nagging, reluctantly took me to test out my new fishing rod.

Nothing had gone right the whole morning. First, Mum left the lights on in the car overnight after returning from night shift, so the battery was flat in the car as we attempted to leave. Once we finally made haste, halfway into our journey, Dad realised he left his wallet on the kitchen counter, and we were fast running out of fuel. By the time we finally got there it was mid-afternoon, the loch painted in grey scale from the dreary clouds above, and there was a westerly breeze blowing a gale. I could tell Dad was simply over it before we began, but he didn't want to let me down.

"All right," he said rather proudly after it had taken us close to an hour to set up the line. "Let's catch a fish, shall we?"

I nodded in excitement, took three steps backwards as I watched him attempt to cast out into the strong prevailing wind.

As if the day couldn't get any worse, when he stepped forward to cast, he slipped on the muddied banks, and slid down into the water, letting out profanity I had never heard escape his lips before.

It was the middle of August and a rather overcast, cold and dreary day with the water close to zero degrees, hardly the most ideal swimming conditions.

"Fuck me," he said, rather annoyed as he brought himself to stand staring down at his saturated and muddied pants.

"Come get the rod, would ye, Finny."

I made my way down to him, carefully but not enough as I too slipped, crashing into Dad, causing him to slip back into the water.

The water was nothing short of bone chilling, but we both burst into hysterics at the absurdity.

We never ended up catching any fish that day, instead electing to make our way back home dirty, wet and cold. It was one of the very few times I heard Dad laugh. I mean, really laugh. The type of laugh that caused my stomach to ache. Not that he was uptight or unhappy. I formed the belief that he preferred not to express his emotions to the degree others did.

The morning I found myself on the shores of the loch for the second time, it couldn't have been more different.

Aside from the weather, which was the clearest day we had seen in weeks, Dad was silent. Present, but only in a physical capacity.

He said absolutely nothing our whole journey, keeping his eyes rigidly fixed out the passenger window in an inaudible glare.

"Do you remember the last time we were here?" I asked him as we pulled into the carpark.

Silence.

"Are you not going to say anything? Dad, please, just fucking say something, anything."

Silence.

In my desperation to connect with him, I felt myself getting irritable. None of this was his fault, but I felt powerless to stop from selfishly inflicting my anger towards him.

"Why are we fucking here, Dad? Tell me!"

I struck the steering wheel in resentment as I peered out to the loch, which looked like a large shard of glass reflecting the blue sky from above.

I felt I was losing him even though Ainsley told me he was still there. How was I meant to see it when he spent his days in silence, leaving me just wanting to hear his voice?

"Dad, I need you. I fucking need you."

He turned and faced me, looking me straight in the

eye. His eyes were fatigued, bloodshot and worn, with a murky grey film accumulating over them. He mouthed something, unable to form the vocals as he brought his hand to his face, shaking his head.

"Dad, can you hear me? Do you even know who I am?" I questioned, my tone still tinged with anger.

He nodded as if to acknowledge me, even if he couldn't vocalise it, and my anger turned to sadness. This wasn't his fault. How could I be such an asshole?

"I'm sorry, I... I just want you back, Dad. God, I just want you back."

He placed his hand over mine as if to offer reassurance he could hear me, and I took the opportunity just to talk, even if I didn't know full well if he tuned in.

That afternoon, we spent hours parked up against the shores of the loch, and I couldn't stop myself from talking. Sharing with him all I had been indebted for in my life thanks to him and even about some of the new equipment we were testing at work. He had always been intrigued about the advancements in military technology, always querying it when I went home on my small pockets of leave.

Sometimes, I found him staring at me as if he was no longer there. His eyes painted with a vagueness that became so familiar. Then there were pockets where I would glance back to find him nodding softly, with a slight smile painted on his lips.

I believed he was there; I needed to believe it.

When I took him back to the facility, it was late afternoon, and they were just starting the dinner rounds.

Ainsley was down the far end of the corridor with another nurse helping a woman into her room.

"I will be with you two shortly," she called out as we reached Dad's door.

A short time later, Ainsley entered the room with a covered plate of food.

"And how was today?" she said, smiling as she took the lid off, revealing a plate of sausages, mashed potatoes, and peas.

"It was fine. I don't think he was with me, though. I tried to believe he was. We just talked, well, I talked," I said, glancing at her with a sombre expression.

"You never know," she said, pouring a cup of water. "Maybe he was even if he couldn't tell you so?"

She wheeled the bed tray over to Dad, who sat upright, vaguely staring out the window, letting out occasional gentle murmurs.

"The most important thing, Finn, how did it make you feel?"

"If I am honest, pretty bloody shit. I lost my temper when I shouldn't have."

"You are only human. I lost my rag with my mother many times. I recall one of the worst times was when I made the mistake of taking her into Aldi, and she halfway through the shop made a scene that I had snatched her wallet."

She let out a laugh, chopping up Dad's sausage. "Finn, I tell ya when we got back to the car after some careful explaining to the supermarket staff, I lost at her. I was upset,

I was embarrassed, and I was furious, not at her, but at the whole situation. I said some unpleasant things to her, Finn, things I still regret to this day. I guess, what I am trying to say is you are human."

"I don't feel like that. I feel like a jackass."

"Well, all I can tell you is it certainly won't be the last time you feel this way."

"Well, that is encouraging, isn't it?" I said, giving her a sardonic smile.

"Where are you going to take him tomorrow?" she questioned, as if in an attempt to change the subject.

"I thought I would take him up the coast for ice cream. We used to always holiday when I was a child in Nairn. He always loved the sea and the beach, despite devoting most of his life out at sea. You would think he would be sick of it. I guess it became like a second home for him in a way."

"That sounds delightful. Did you hear that? You're going to the beach tomorrow. Aren't ye lucky!"

She tried to get him to eat something, but he turned his head in objection.

"Come on now, you need all the energy you can for your adventure tomorrow," she said, smiling in her jovial tone.

"How are you always so positive?"

"Well, how else am I meant to be? Gloomy? Depressed? What fun would that be? This place already is a stone's throw from emotional hell for most people."

"Sorry, that wasn't an insult. I find it, I find you...

Well, you are refreshing. Let's put it that way."

"I didn't see it as an insult."

A period of silence passed before Ainsley cleared her throat, glancing at me twice as if hesitant.

"Do you want to grab something to eat? A decent meal?"

"What is classed as a decent meal?" I joked, seizing the opportunity to inject some humour.

"One where someone cooks for you," she smirked as she walked around to the front of the bed to slip some compression stockings over Dad's legs.

"Do you want me to cook for you?" I joked again, as I could see she was getting uncomfortable.

"Finn, for crying out loud, do you have to? I am trying to be sincere here."

"And you're saying I am not?"

Strangely, I had the impression she wasn't asking for conversation's sake, or even because she was particularly interested in me. Rather, I sensed she was asking because she was curious for her own reasons, whatever those might be.

"Well, I..."

"It's a date."

I could tell my attempt at a joke infuriated her as she cast me a wide-eyed stare.

"Finn, I am not asking you for a date. I want your company to appreciate a nice meal since you are the closest thing to a friend I have at the moment."

I smirked, choosing to test the limitations of her humour.

"Sounds like a date."

"Oh, stop it or I will revoke my invitation." She placed her hands on her hips, her lips slightly separated, and I wasn't entirely sure if she was about to burst out laughing or attempt to hit me.

"Ok, I will stop," I said, laughing, jokingly shielding my face.

"When do you want to go?"

"How about..." she paused as she went silent for a moment before glancing at me with a wry smile. "How about tonight?"

"You don't give me much warning, do you? I can see you don't do this often."

"Are you making fun of me?"

"No, of course not."

She continued to stare at me. "I think you are."

"Okay, maybe a little."

She thought about my answer as she finally gave up trying to get Dad to eat. "Well, I guess I will meet you there."

"No, no, that just won't do. I will pick you up."

"No, I will meet you there as this is not a date."

"If you say so." I laughed, watching her cheeks become a deeper shade of mauve pink.

"Finn..."

"Ainsley…"

"I'm meeting you there. End of the story."

I could tell I had to admit defeat. If anything, I learned about Ainsley over the last few weeks, was that she didn't take the lay down approach in life. "As you wish, my lady."

Dad was silent minus his loud, rattled breathing. "Dad, I am going to head off now, all right?" I said, making my way over to him as he stared out the window.

"I will come and see you tomorrow, and we are going to hit the beach!"

I tried to sound humorous, but I thought the escapades would become more harmful to me emotionally than good. The visit to the loch filled me with further resentment for the situation we found ourselves in, despite the intention of being the complete opposite.

"Tomorrow will be a better day, I am sure," Ainsley said as she walked over to the window to pull the blinds.

"I'm not convinced."

"Well, if you ain't got hope, you ain't got much, do you now?" Perhaps she was right, but my hope for the situation was fading fast.

Changes

Part of what made me a good soldier was that I was always punctual and observant, but as of late, my timings left a lot to be desired. My punctuality was becoming fleeting, and I no longer recognised myself in the mirror. The evening I arranged to meet with Ainsley, I fell asleep on the couch, exhausted from the week's events. My peaceful slumber abruptly ended when my phone rang loudly from the gap between the two aged brown sofa cushions.

"Fuck," I said as I peered at the illuminated screen, realising it was just after 7:00pm and I was meant to be meeting Ainsley.

"Hello," I answered, knowing it was her calling, and feeling anxious to speak with her, afraid she'd be upset with me for my tardiness.

Before she responded, I could hear the background noise of patrons muffled in the distance. "Finn, where are you?" There was a less than impressed tone to her voice.

"Ainsley, I am so sorry. I fell asleep." I was already up and moving, trying to gather myself to get ready, but not wanting her to think I was busy elsewhere and intending to stand her up.

"We can reschedule if tonight no longer suits," she replied with a tenderness in her voice that helped me relax.

She, of all people, could understand what I was going through.

"No, no, I won't be long," I laughed, scanning the room for a clean shirt.

"Where do you live?" She paused before she rephrased the question. "I mean, are you close to here?"

"Twenty minutes or so."

"I'll come and get you because there are far too many people around for me to stand here awkwardly for that long."

"So does that mean it is a date, then?" I joked, knowing it would irritate her.

"Shut up, Finn. You are not half as funny as you think you are."

I relayed my address and directions to her before we ended the call, and I raced to get ready.

A short time later, after I managed a quick shower, throwing on a white, red, and blue linen plaid shirt and jeans, Ainsley turned up at my doorstep wearing a short black dress and a red woollen coat. It was a stark contrast to the shapeless, pale blue scrubs I recognised her in, so I couldn't help but stare.

"Wow," I said out loud while I studied her. "You look great."

"I don't look like a twelve-year-old boy all the time, you know," she said, her cheeks blushing as she giggled. A sound that was becoming one of my favourite things to hear.

"Are you ready?"

"Well, I feel underdressed now," I replied as I glanced at my jeans.

"You look fine. Hurry; it's freezing out here."

As we made our way to the steakhouse, I couldn't help but glance at her every few seconds. In the time we had spent together, of course, I recognised her natural beauty, but I never noticed she was outright stunning. The fluorescent lights of the care home didn't do her justice because even in the dim light cast on her as we made our way to the restaurant, I could see she's gorgeous.

Over dinner, I came to learn more about her. How she grew up in Ireland on the poverty line and the aspirations she held for the future. "I want a house in the country. Maybe somewhere in Aberdeenshire. Not a big house, just a cottage with a nice garden."

"Do you know much about gardening?" I questioned, taking a sip of my pint.

Her eyes drifted to the servers moving around in a well-choreographed dance, dodging each other without spilling a drop. "No, but I would like to."

"My father said once you start gardening, time becomes a currency you can never get enough of."

"Just as well. Outside of work I have plenty of time." She ran her hand around the lip of her wineglass.

"Can I ask you something?" I wanted to know more about how she got through the battle with her own mother as I was feeling increasingly overwhelmed by my father's.

"Sure."

"How did you get through it?"

"Losing my mother?"

"Aye." I held my breath, unsure if my question was obnoxious or not.

She didn't seem to mind as she gave me a brief smile, her head tilted slightly. "I guess it was just a time thing. For a long time, I was really lost. My ma, well she was all I really had because me and Niall had broken up. For six or seven months, I was downright miserable and why I made the choice to come over here. A fresh start, a new beginning."

I nodded, panning the bar, unsure of where to look, feeling her eyes on me.

"I am scared of losing him like this. All he wanted was to be a grandfather. I feel I disappointed him given my failure in that regard."

"Do you want kids?" Ainsley questioned, her voice sounding curious.

I thought about her question, staring at her as she gazed at me with her pale green eyes. If she asked me a year ago, I would have said definitely not, but the experience with my father changed me. In all his achievements in life, he always maintained I was his greatest and, in many ways, I felt I had let him down. "I'm undecided on that one. Yourself?"

She swirled the wine in her glass. "I think so, but I mean, I find the prospect oddly, well, terrifying."

"You find children terrifying?" I was amused. "You are an odd one."

She laughed, throwing her head back, and I realised, given the euphoric sensation it gave me, I enjoyed talking to her. It was easy and natural, unlike with so many other people I experienced.

She must have laughed too hard as she grabbed her nose to prevent the liquid that had been snorted in her laughter from escaping her nostrils.

I looked away to prevent myself from bursting out into an uncontrollable fit of laughter.

"Quit laughing at me," she said, studying my expression.

My eyes lingered on her lower lip for a moment, and I couldn't stop myself from thinking how soft it looked. "I'm not laughing."

"I can see it in your face. You're laughing on the inside."

If only she knew how I was feeling on the inside. If I knew. "All right, I'll stop." I smirked as I watched her fumble in her purse.

She pulled a tissue from her handbag, dabbing her under eyes. "Good. So, tell me, what else?"

"What else what?"

"What else can you tell me about yourself?" she asked as she continued to hold the tissue to her nose.

"I don't know. What do you want to know?"

"Tell me something no one else knows about you."

I took a moment to contemplate how vulnerable I was willing to be with her, but all of my instincts told me there was no truth I could share that she would judge me for. Yet, I started small. "I'm scared of the dark."

"Finn, I am being serious," she said with a scornful glare.

"So am I." Shifting my eyes to the tented dessert menu placed on the edge of our table, I held my breath, waiting for her to reply.

Her expression changed. Perhaps she was unsure of how to react. Her blank expression left a world of uncertainty.

"It's fine. I shouldn't joke about it. Since I came back from deployment, it's just been something I have learnt to deal with. I guess I just need to know where I am at all times."

She paused, as if trying to organise her chaotic thoughts. "I forget you are military sometimes. You seem far different from any military men I have ever met."

"Oh really? How many military men have you been around?" I smirked at her, curious about her encounters with military personnel. Desperate to know if their impressions on her would somehow impact her opinion of me.

"Not many," she said with an awkward laugh. "Like, one. A friend's brother in Ireland." With a pause, she turned her attention to her glass. "What was it like? Over there I mean. I've heard absolute horror stories."

"Everyone's experience is different. I guess it is hard to vocalise it, but it changed me." I wasn't uncomfortable, but somehow, I winced, knowing she was probably going to question me for details when it wasn't something I wanted to discuss, especially not in a crowded bar.

She saw my expression but misinterpreted it. "I'm sorry if I made you uncomfortable," she whispered. "I do that sometimes. Act too forward, I mean. I just blurt out what I'm thinking without considering how it might come across to others."

"You didn't make me uncomfortable," I said, turning my face to hers. "It's just not something any of us really talk about." I almost stopped there, aware that if I kept the words inside, the moment would pass, but I told her about Blair. "I've lost several friends, Ainsley, over the last two years," I began. "Blair confided in me he is struggling now, too. I want to give him my attention but my father's time, we both know it is fast becoming borrowed."

I always imagined the words would be hard to say, but they weren't. In all my life, I'd never openly discussed anything, but somehow, she relaxed me. I felt she understood me in ways others didn't, even though we had just met.

"I don't think anybody would hold it against you, Finn, giving your father your attention for now. As for Blair, well," she took another pause, sipping her wine. "Do you think he will be okay?" There was a sense of sincerity evident in her voice as she focused on me.

I was unsure. All I could do was hope that he would get the support I knew he needed, even if he didn't recognise it. "Aye. I think he has a partner and supportive family. Anyway, back to you. What is something nobody knows about you?"

She mulled over my question as she held my gaze. "Well, I'm scared that I will die alone. With, I must add, a whole heap of cats."

I couldn't help but laugh at the imagery. Ainsley, the beautiful, kind-hearted, determined woman in front of me, surrounded by enough shelter cats to warrant her own reality TV show. "In your cottage with the garden?"

"Yes, in my cottage with my garden." She laughed with a grin. "Thanks, Finn, I..." she hesitated, her voice gentle. "I really enjoyed tonight; I needed a good laugh."

I would never admit it as freely as she did that night, but her feelings were reciprocated. I couldn't remember the last time I laughed so hard, let alone shared so openly.

As the bar drew close, we made our way outside, where a soft drizzle began to fall.

"Can you drive? Because I cannot," she said, her arms outstretched with her head tilted back. "Do you like the rain? I love the rain. It always feels so invigorating."

I stared at her, sliding on my coat, amused at the mildly drunk tone in her voice. "How many glasses did you have?"

"Hmm, three, four? Maybe five? I actually can't remember," she replied before she erupted into laughter.

"Clearly enough." I joked, hailing down a taxi as it came down the road.

"Should we drop you off first?" I queried once we slid across the smooth leather seats under cover from the rain. The air was tinged with the smell of peppermint and cigarettes and the faintest hint of Ainsley's perfume.

"Yes, I have work tomorrow." She giggled, resting her head up against the side window.

"You are going to feel so great tomorrow."

"Self-inflicted torment, I love me a bit of that." She giggled again, and I felt a pang in my chest, not ready to say goodbye to that for the night.

We sat in silence during the five-minute drive to her flat, deep in our own wayward thoughts – at least, I know mine were. The silence was ended by the taxi driver signalling he would have to park down the street.

"It's fine, Finn, you stay here. I'll run."

I looked down at her heels. "You cannot run in those."

"Watch me." She tilted her head to the right with a widespread grin.

An idea sprang to my mind, which was terrible but would give me a few more moments in her presence. "You are a hazard to those things. Come here, I'll carry you."

"You most certainly will not. I am far too heavy for that." She opened her door, pausing as if to wait for my reply before standing.

"Ainsley, come on. You are what, five stone?"

"Do I really look like a twelve-year-old boy to you? Even so. Absolutely not."

I felt she was annoyed at my comment, and I couldn't let what was a wonderful evening end that way. "Come on, I do this all the time for combat med training."

"All right then," she said reluctantly, as I scooped her up and ran towards her door.

She couldn't contain her hysterics as we ran in the pouring rain.

Before I placed her down, there was a moment where we both stared at each other, intoxicated but aware all the same.

"Thank you," she said, her voice softened, face drenched from the rain.

"Anytime," I laughed before I placed her down.

"Finn, do…" she stammered as she let out a laugh. "Do you want to come inside?" I knew by the fluster in her voice she desired me just as much as I did her, but I knew it would be a mistake. She was my father's nurse and fast becoming a good friend. A moment of lust had the potential to derail a relationship I valued. It wasn't a risk I was willing to take, even though I wanted to.

"Beach day with Dad tomorrow." I smiled, doing my best attempt to wipe the rain from my forehead to change the subject.

"That's right," she said, bending down to straighten her dress with a smile.

I could sense an element of disappointment in her tone and part of me was resisting every urge not to take up her offer, knowing exactly where it would lead.

"I'll see you tomorrow?" I said politely as she unlocked her door.

"You most certainly will," she said, turning back to face me. "Thanks again, it was fun."

Nairn

Nairn, a little over two-hour drive north, will always be somewhere that holds fond memories for me. It was a place we went often as a family in the summer to escape the city and relax. It has the infamous title of the sunniest place in Scotland, and the day my father and I arrived did not disappoint. We arrived just past noon, with my father sitting in silence the entire journey from Aberdeen. For October, the weather remained unusually warm, the sun high, and the sky illustrated in a deep blue as he sat watching the sea churn the sand.

I stared at the sandy dunes that held memories of my childhood, reminiscing, and realising I hadn't been there for over a decade. As I dredged my father's wheelchair through the pale sand, it felt like little had changed, which, for a fleeting moment, was a nice change from the reality of knowing everything was different.

"Dad, do you remember when we came here the summer before I went to high school?" I asked him as I wrapped a blanket over his thinning legs.

To my surprise, he responded and murmured in agreement before he pointed to a vague outline of a ship in the distance.

"Aye, nice to see ye eyes still work, Da." I gave him a

gentle pat on the knee before taking a seat in the white sand one would usually associate with a tropical paradise.

After a week of minimal lucidity, it was comforting to hear his voice. Given my growing concern I never would again.

"I remember," he said, his voice a soft tremble. Even though he was having a moment of lucidity, his voice was weak. He replied the best he could, but his breath became laboured.

"Do you remember trying to impress Ma, coming out of the sea trying to look like James Bond only to get knocked over by a wave. When you stood up, there was blood everywhere. You were exposed when your shorts slid down and you were a wreck."

He smiled with a rasped chuckle. "I still impressed her though." His smile as he recalled the memory had tears welling in my eyes. He remembered. "I miss her," he mumbled, staring out to sea.

I paused, following his gaze. "So do I, Da. So do I."

"You were in such a foul frame of mind that day." He was struggling to finish his sentence, but selfishly, this is the most he had spoken in some time, and I didn't want to discourage him.

"Was I?" My recollection of the day was vague, so his comment surprised me.

"Yes, you were. You wanted to go visit some girl also on holiday and we said no."

"Who?" I laughed.

"Her name might have been Jenny or Ginny."

I realised then who Dad had been talking about, even though for the life of me I couldn't fathom how he even remembered. Ginny Wilton moved onto our street a month before our visit that summer. I soon developed a crush on her after I found out she liked soccer more than she enjoyed writing in journals and painting her nails. Ginny and Blair never got along. Blair became convinced it was because she liked him, but I held my ideas they were just too much alike.

Ginny, just like Blair, had a mop of red hair and a loud, charismatic personality – something I thought Blair sometimes regarded as threatening. Her family owned a small seaside cottage in Nairn, which they visited in the summers, like us. She told me she would give me a kiss if I snuck out to meet her at the beach. At twelve, I thought if I hadn't kissed a girl by then, I would be doomed, so I looked at that opportunity as my only hope. The night I agreed to meet Ginny, I found my mother seated downstairs with a glass of whisky. I became convinced she could read my thoughts.

"Where do you think you are going?" I heard her voice as I slipped on my shoes.

I don't think my heart has ever jolted in my chest so violently from panic in my life. I turned to my left to see my mother in her dressing gown with a smirk painted across her face.

"I was, I was..." I stammered, trying to fling my shoe off my foot.

"You were going to see that girl, weren't you?" She raised her glass to her lips, taking a sip and setting it down in a move that reminded me of an old-fashioned gangster movie.

"No," I said, my voice tinged with panic.

"Finn, I know you." She laughed, forming wrinkles at the side of her eyes.

"Please don't tell Dad," I mumbled.

There was a moment's pause before I heard a bout of laughter from behind me, realising my father witnessed the full conversation.

That night became the first and only time they ever grounded me in my whole life, and it would become something they never let me live down.

"I can't believe you remember that," I said, turning my attention to a couple as they walked hand in hand down the beach.

"I know, it is getting worse," he replied, his voice solemn.

His awareness both surprised and confused me. "What do you mean?"

Staring at his feet, he continued, "I'm aware there are more bad days than good."

"You are here today, though. That is all that matters."

He shook his head as he let out a heaved sigh, which crackled as it trailed. "I never dreamed I would go out like this."

I turned to study his face; the dry, weathered skin folded into a displeased stare. "Nobody is going anywhere yet, Da."

"But eventually I will, Finn. I know this; you know

this."

Broaching a conversation about what was realistically going to happen was not how I wanted to spend that day. "Let's not think about that right now, eh?" I said as I brought myself to stand, dusting the sand that had stuck itself to my jeans. "Let's see how cold that water is."

We made our way down to the water's edge, the tide on its way out. My calves were burning from the sheer force of having to move my father in the thick, soft sand. I slid my shoes off, neatly tucking them in the undercarriage of his wheelchair, and rolled up my jeans.

"My turn," my father said with a sly smile, removing the blanket from his legs.

"Da, it's a terrible idea. You might get sick," I replied, knowing his immunity had become near absent. Having him out in the elements was enough of a risk.

"Finn, you know just as much as I that I will never get the chance again."

I bent down, slid his slippers from his feet, and rolled his cream-coloured trousers up to his knees. With my attention diverted, I didn't see a rogue wave coming in our direction until we were hit with it, saturating us in freezing cold salty water.

My father, who said very little in the weeks prior, erupted in laughter, running his hands over his face, tasting the salt with his tongue.

"Well, that will do it," I said, drying my eyes.

"Take me out further, Finn, I want to feel it again."

"Da..."

"Finn, please."

I wheeled him out far enough that each wave licked the bottom of his foot pedals. Each time, he broke out into an absurd cackle of laughter. I was terrified. Not of the water – but of the impact it could have on him.

It didn't matter what others thought, and I guessed we received a few glares. Two grown men, one in a wheelchair in fits of amusement in the freezing cold sea. For the first time in a long time, my father seemed happy. The veil of his sickness had fled, even if for a fleeting moment. I could do nothing but stare at him and smile, his face lit by his sheer wonder, and my fear morphed into happiness watching him live.

He knew, and I knew, we would never go back there again, but it didn't matter. At that moment, the air saturated with his joy; I knew it was everything it should have been.

When we arrived back at the facility, we were met with questions about why both of us had soaking wet clothes. I removed Dad's pants and wrapped him in the blanket for our journey home. As I wheeled him into the facility with his wet pants slung over the handles, the wheels still embedded with sand, we copped multiple displeased glares.

"How was it?" Ainsley asked as she greeted us in the hallway, her eyes darting between my father and I.

"Great," Dad replied before I had time to.

"Well, that is something," she smiled, and opened the door to his room. "We best get you changed then." Ainsley took over as she wheeled him to the left of his bed, helping him up. "Was the weather good?"

"It was lovely, much warmer than here," I replied, staring at the dark grey skies forming in the distance.

"It's forecast to rain." After our dinner date, the forced small talk felt awkward. I wasn't content with neutral conversation anymore.

"Welcome to Aberdeen, it always rains." I laughed in response. "How are you feeling?"

She slid off Dad's top, reaching for a clean linen gown to her left. "How am I? Well, I never want to drink wine again," she said, her eyes widened.

"Is it that bad?"

"It is that bad." She laughed.

"What a shame. I actually considered asking you again." I levelled her with a smirk and I could tell she was trying to remain professional.

"Is that so?" she said, sounding amused. "I might have to rethink that."

My father stared at me as if he was deep in thought, trying to establish the sincerity of our discussion as Ainsley gently slid a gown over his head.

"How are you feeling?" Ainsley said as she brought herself down to my father's eye level.

He smiled, not saying a word.

"You look chilly. How about we get you tucked up into bed now?" She helped him into bed, pulling a warm blanket up to just below his chin. "Would you like a cup of tea?"

"Is he okay?" I questioned, alarmed by his sudden onset of silence.

"I think so, just tired." Ainsley glanced over her shoulder in my direction. "It would have been a big day for him."

I nodded as I watched her pour him a cup of tea before placing it on his bedside table.

"Thank you."

"Thank you for what?" She turned around in surprise.

"Just, you know, you have been so good with him."

"Well, I have to admit, so far he is one of my favourites. I do really love his stories."

"I guess I better go." I realised the time, knowing that visiting hours were coming to a close.

There was a moment's silence as we both looked at each other before Ainsley cleared her throat. "I'll walk you out."

In the hallway's privacy, we made our way towards the exit door. Both of us had one question on our mind, made clear when we both said the same thing.

"Finn, do you...?"

"Ainsley do you...?"

Our voices crossed over each other as we both laughed.

"I have a day off tomorrow." Her words came out with conviction, but her eyes were directed at the floor.

I hesitated, trying to think of what to say without

sounding too eager.

"Do you want to do something?" she questioned before I got the chance.

"Okay, I would like that. Should I pick you up?"

She laughed as she shook her head. "No, because that would make it a date."

"Of course, well, we can't have that now," I replied as I opened the door.

"See you tomorrow."

That evening, I called and checked in on Blair. Since the conversation in the bar with Ainsley, he played heavily on my mind. My guilty conscience was pulling me to invest more energy into helping him, knowing I was likely one of the one people in the world who would understand it. As selfish as it seemed, I struggled with the concept, knowing it would make me revisit an old wound myself which had the potential to derail me. My father needed me to be present, yet I felt guilty for wanting to spend time with Ainsley. Not that she was more important than him. Her presence in my life helped calm me when the situation with my father felt overwhelming.

I groaned into my pillow, feeling the weight of my head getting pulled in all directions before I reached for my phone.

When Blair answered, I could tell things weren't great, but I didn't press it.

"What are ye plans tomorrow?" I questioned, prepared to drop plans with Ainsley if he had been free.

"Me and Shell are going to look at houses."

"Aye, well should we go for a drink Thursday?"

He didn't reply straight away, which was unusual. "Ye righto Finny," he finally said.

"Are ye sure yew all right?" I questioned.

"I'm right. Just knackered."

Even though part of me was nagging to press him further, I respected he didn't want to talk.

"Aye, rest up."

"Will do, Finny, see ye Thursday."

Ben Rinnes

Overnight, the skies opened up, releasing a deluge of rain and loud thunder. I barely slept, lying awake with my thoughts all over the place. Unaware when I drifted off, I awoke the following morning by the sound of two text messages from Ainsley.

"What time is it?" I groaned, reaching for my phone.

You are fit, right?

What kind of question was that? I yawned, bringing myself to stand by a stretch. My head felt like it had been hit by a freight train, so for a split second, I considered cancelling.

I want to take a walk. I was thinking maybe we could do Ben Rimes. I am told it is best to do it this time of the year.

Ben Rimes? She had to be joking. Today of all days? The last time I was up to Ben Rimes was when my mother made her bucket list after her diagnosis. She insisted on climbing every mountain in Scotland with me as her companion.

I hope you are joking. I replied before placing my phone down on the tallboy dresser, pulling my curtains open to expose the morning light. She has to be joking, I thought, looking at the concrete-coloured sky.

My phone vibrated again with her reply, and I anticipated her answer with an accelerated heart rate. Her attention made me feel things I hadn't felt in... well, ever.

No, I am dead serious. I have checked the weather and we are good to go. I will pick you up in an hour.

I let out a laugh at her revelation. Live in Scotland long enough and you will come to know the weather forecasts are never truly accurate.

Ben Rimes was a mountain on the Moray coast. It was a three-hour journey, give or take, and I had done no form of physical activity for a month; the very thought of it filled me with dread. Once I showered and changed, Ainsley showed up at my door dressed in a top to toe mountaineering kit.

"We aren't climbing Everest," I joked, laughing at her attire.

"Better to be prepared," she shrugged, her voice sounding unimpressed.

"That is more than prepared."

She looked at me up and down in my shorts, thermal top and shirt with a disgruntled stare. "Well, you are not just wearing that, are you?"

"Yes? Do I need to remind you I grew up here?"

"You have to take a jacket."

"No. What are you, my mother?"

"Finn, you are taking a jacket." She replied more firmly. I found her mildly authoritative tone amusing as she stood staring at me with her left hand on her hip.

"Are you always so bossy?"

It took her a long time to answer. "No," she murmured. "I'm not."

"Well, I guess since you insist," I said as I sarcastically rolled my eyes before grabbing a jacket from my coat stand.

Just under two months before my mother passed, she had two mountains left to tick off her list. Ben Rimes and Ben Lomond. She woke me early on one particular Saturday with a look of determination on her face after having a rough week of nausea and fatigue. She already spent two days that week in hospital, so it came with concerned surprise that she decided that day would be perfect to tick off one of the two mountains left.

"Ceemon ye," she said, jumping on the bed like a child the night before Christmas.

"Ceemon what, ma?" I replied with a groan, doing my best attempt to shield my face from the morning light streaming into the room.

"We are going for a walk."

"We are? Whose decision is that? Mine or yours?"

"Come on Finn, get your arse up!"

I sat myself upright and stared at her. "Are you sure you are up to walking, ma? It has been a bad week." I knew the answer she would give me but somehow asked anyway, hoping she would reconsider.

"No excuses. C'mon let's go."

No matter how sick she became, she never lost her determination. The day we climbed up was less than ideal given it poured with rain an hour into our ascent, but she insisted we continue.

"Ma, I think we should go back." I turned around and yelled out to her, squinting from the rain seeping into my eyes. The rain became so heavy that the narrow rocky path became a torrential stream, each step splashing muddied water in all directions.

"No, we are nearly there," she replied, pushing past me with a gentle nudge to walk ahead.

As if it was meant to be, once we got to the top of the summit, the rain cleared, revealing a gap of blue sky and we could see all the way out to the Moray Coast, the coastline painted in a dark grey.

"I did it," she exclaimed with a wide grin. "Come here, you," she instructed, embracing me in an impressively strong hug.

"Ye are a bloody cracker, ye are ma," I replied, taking a moment to catch my breath.

There was a moment of silence as we both tried to soothe our lungs.

"Promise me something, Finn," she said with several large wheezy breaths.

"Depends on what I am promising."

She looks at me with a displeased stare at my answer before wiping her saturated face on her sleeve. "No matter how bad it gets, please do your best to stay by his side."

"Ma, of course I…"

"No, listen to me," she said firmly, raising her hand as if to interrupt me.

"It will get ugly Finn, I mean it. You haven't seen the things I have. It will get ugly, and it will be hard, really hard. I know I won't live long enough to help ease the burden, so I need you to promise me."

"Of course, I promise."

The day I found myself there with Ainsley, I couldn't help but laugh at Ainsley's determined face bearing a striking resemblance to the exact face my mother wore in the same place many months earlier.

"How long do you think it will take?" She questioned tying her shoelace as we stood in the carpark, staring up towards the summit.

"It usually takes three hours."

"I reckon we can do it in two," she replied with a smirk.

"You have got to be joking." My wide eyes didn't deter her in the slightest.

"Nay, Finny. I am dead serious." There was a hint of mischievousness in her tone which had me intrigued, ready to follow her just to see if she could achieve her lofty goal.

Before I could reason with her, she made her way up the track in a light jog. "Come on now, we haven't got all day."

Part of me considered jumping back in the car and waiting for her to return, but I succumbed, reluctantly chasing after her.

Once we got to the top, both red faced with our lungs heaving, we took a seat on a smoothed rock staring at the foothills below.

"It really is quite pretty," she remarked, taking several laboured breaths. Her heavy breathing was justified, because she made excellent time to the top.

"My mum always thought there was something special about this place, she always felt it had a presence." I stared out at the horizon, soaking in the beauty my mother insisted on seeing. Trying to feel connected with her, this place was the setting for one of our last days together.

"It does. Don't you think?"

I nodded, taking a sip of my water. "Aye, it does."

"What was she like? Your father's stories, they really are a laugh."

"My mother? She was a good woman." I stared out at the landscape, remembering my mother and all the inspiring qualities she possessed.

"She sounded it."

"She dragged me up here before she died. She made a bucket list to climb every mountain in Scotland."

"Every mountain?"

"Every mountain. We did Ben Lomond about two weeks before she passed." I smiled, feeling my eyes water from the memory. "I was hesitant as I worried the cold would make her sick. She was already so weak towards the end there, but she insisted. She only walked about thirty minutes, then I carried her the rest of the way. It was the most gorgeous day."

"You carried her?"

"Aye, I did. Slung her over my shoulders. She laughed most of the way. I tell ya, if I can be half the person she was, then it will be a life well lived."

Ainsley paused, giving me a soft smile.

"I think you are well on your way there Finn, I don't know you that well but the way your father spoke of you I feel they were both very proud of you."

Ainsley diverted her gaze to a couple making their way down the track. "I apologise for all the questions. Your father, well, he talks about both of you a lot."

"Does he?"

"He does. How they met and that she would cook the best yorkshire puddings. It was something my mother used to do too."

"Well, I will give him something. He isn't wrong. She really was the best. What was your mother like?"

"My mother," Ainsley replied with a soft chuckle. "She was hard Finn, very hard. Smoke a packet a day, drink a bottle of whisky every two days. She had dreams and aspirations she never got to fulfil, and I think in a way it made her bitter." She closed her eyes, nodding her head slightly in thought. "She made me want to do something with my life. Don't get me wrong, Finn. I loved her and she loved me more than life itself, but our relationship had its complexity because I only ever wanted her to grasp her life and want better for herself."

"Seems like she did okay," I replied, walking closer to the edge.

"Okay with me?"

"Who else would I be talking about?" I said, amused.

"I have my issues, Finn; we aren't without our issues."

"Aye, but you have your head screwed on at least."

"Can I ask you something?" Ainsley questioned as she slid off her jacket, stuffing it into her dark blue backpack.

"Depends on what it is." I laughed, glancing over my shoulder in her direction and recalling my mother's similar open-ended request.

Looking out at the horizon, she responded, "Well, if that is the case..."

"Go on, you can't backtrack now." For an unexplainable reason, I had the urge to reach out and grab her hand, but I knew that could turn a friendly hike into more.

She paused, chewing on her lip nervously. "You said you hadn't met the right one?"

"As in partner?"

She nodded, saying nothing.

"Why does everyone seem so convinced that relationships equal happiness?" Suddenly feeling the urge that I needed space, I walked to the opposite edge from her. A stark contrast to the feelings I was having moments earlier.

"I never said that." She stood up, brushing the light dusting of dirt on her knees to the ground.

"But you most certainly are thinking about it."

Ainsley walked several steps forward, lost in her thoughts. I waited, somehow knowing she would break the silence. "I mean, don't you get lonely?" she finally asked as she turned around.

"I could ask you the same thing."

She laughed. "Don't do that."

"Don't do what?"

"Bring me into the equation."

"Act surprised I was going to ask that question."

She raised an eyebrow. "All I am thinking, before you wonder, is whether we're actually friends. Because friends are honest with each other. You hold a lot of secrets, I can tell. My only question is, what is holding you back?"

"I am here, aren't I?" I say with a shrug, ignoring her real question.

Without displaying an ounce of bitterness at me dodging what she'd asked, she replied, "You might just feel sorry for me."

"Well, you said it. Not me." Though I resisted the idea, I had to admit she intrigued me. Not because of the things she had done for me, as touching as that was. It was more to do with the sad way she smiled sometimes, her expression when she talked about her mother. There was a loneliness within her she couldn't disguise, and I knew it matched my own.

"I need to sit down," I said, breaking the silence and changing the subject before we dived into a conversation we couldn't return from.

Ainsley hesitated before taking a seat next to me.

Close enough so the fibres of our clothing touched. I reached for my pack, pulling out my fluorescent green drink bottle, taking a chug of water.

"I find you, well, interesting," I said with a smirk.

"Interesting? Is that your way of a compliment?" She questioned, reaching for her own bottle.

"Well, you can take that any way you want."

"Well, I find you hard work."

"Hard work?" I glanced at her, and my eyes widened.

"Yes, very much so."

We both sat in silence, staring out at the foothills that became painted in a fine evening mist. For the first time, I recognised that there was a feeling between us; something that felt foreign and uncomfortable starting to burn deep within my layers. It was irrational and illogical, going against everything I had ever promised myself. I glanced at her while she stared out at the vast rolling green hills below and I realised I wanted to know her. I wanted to understand her.

Photographs

Early after my father was diagnosed, Dr Wells relayed to me the benefit of using photographs to connect with him. At the time I didn't understand, questioning to myself how it could be any use if he was forgetting everything.

"See Finn, when you lose your memory, you lose your sense of self. This isn't just limited to our personal identity, but at what part of the road we are on in life. There have been several studies done that visual aids help stimulate memories for those with dementia, regardless of where they are in their progression."

"Visual aids as in photos?" I questioned as I watched him flicking through my father's file. The day prior, my father had undertaken his normal routine checks of blood and a CT scan to assess the progressiveness of his disease.

"Photos and even books, Finn. Image association through photos and images can help stimulate memories."

"Won't it upset him?" I questioned.

"I think you will find quite the opposite."

When my mother gave up her passion for drawing to pursue her career in nursing, she found a new love in photography. Photo albums one after another, she filled them. I underestimated just how many until I found myself in the attic the following day after meeting with Dr Wells looking for them.

At the back of the attic behind an old mahogany Victorian dresser I came across several boxes taped shut, one which when I laid my eyes on gave me a sense of familiarity. I ran my hands over the pale blue box, realising it was the one I had seen my father with all those years ago. As I gently peeled back the paper-coloured tape, I breathed a sigh of the dusty churned air. I only had a vague recollection of what was inside as I slid the lid off, revealing several items, including a small photo album at the bottom. The plastic film that encased each photo dissolved into crumbling pieces; the photos remained discoloured but intact. I studied his face, a boy that never grew into a man feeling a wave of emotion surge through me I had never encountered before.

Perhaps it was because of my heightened emotions at the time given the week that transpired with my father, but I shed uncontrollable tears. All those years ago I was robbed of a brother, one who no doubt would've made me feel less alone in the situation I found myself in. The unfairness of it all wasn't something I had ever given much thought to, but oddly, staring at his unfamiliar face, I questioned who he could have become and how life could have been different.

I eventually found the albums hidden in the next book, all thirteen of them, and made my way to visit Dad.

When I arrived, he was seated with his bed inclined, staring out the window in a vague stare. "Morning Dad, how are we?" I asked, knowing I would not get a reply, but I at least hoped he would hear me.

Silence.

"I brought something to show you," I said, pulling the first photo album from my bag. It had a brown case with a gold trim and when I flicked open to the first page, I realised it was likely a collection of photographs from when I was roughly eight years old.

I pulled my chair closer to him, lifting the photo album to meet his gaze. "Do you remember her?" I questioned as I pointed to a picture of my mother standing knee deep in snow. She looked so youthful with her red hair tied back into a loose, messy bun and a smile spread across her face.

He studied the photograph in silence. In the photo, she looked elegant and autonomous, the strong-willed woman who'd captured his heart, and I could tell he was trying to piece it together. "Bonnie?" he questioned, his voice brittle.

I grinned as I watched him study the picture. A soft smile spread across his face.

"My Bonnie."

"Aye, you are right there, Dad. That's Mum."

He nodded, running his fingers over the photo. "She was so beautiful."

"She was, wasn't she?" I replied, turning the page.

On the next page were several photos of when we spent Easter with my father's older brother, Neville. Before he migrated to the Shetlands with Shirley, he worked on a sizable farm on the shores of Loch Linnhe. Neville lost his first wife Mabel when my cousin Graeme was just an infant in a freak accident. She fell from her horse when trying to ride across a ridge on the farm. We all assumed he would never remarry as the accident hardened him. Unlike my father, who was meticulous in his presentation, my uncle was rough, unshaven, and cursed more than he should. When Graeme was six, he met Shirley, a woman neither my mother nor father particularly liked. To me, she seemed fine, but I would often hear my mother and father express how they thought she was manipulative and narcissistic in personality. While my father and Neville became estranged when he eventually married Shirley for a vast amount of my childhood, we would often visit. My mother hated visiting them both and not simply because she didn't like Shirley. She was convinced the large six-bedroom Georgian homestead was haunted, never able to sleep when we were there. I experienced nothing that would prove so. Even though my cousin Graeme would often relay stories of things heard and seen, the factualness of his stories remained debatable.

"Look, there's you, da." I laughed as I pointed to a picture of my father trying to wrangle a sheep covered in mud.

"I remember that day."

"Do you?" I questioned as I looked at him, astonished.

"Aye, I do."

At the time, Graeme was nursing a broken ankle after falling from a ladder doing roof repairs. It was the heart of lambing season and the sheep in question had struggled to birth. Graeme gave my father a brief whistle training to get his two collies to do the work to secure her in the yard. My father had other ideas, getting impatient as the dogs got confused by his unrecognisable attempts at command.

"This is useless, I'm just going to do it myself," he said heatedly before he ran towards the sheep with his hand outstretched.

It was pouring, and between me, Mum and him, we were over it. Aberdeen wasn't known for the most desirable weather but could count on one hand over all the years I had been there, the sunny days I experienced.

"You are going to make it worse," my mother called out, observing from the shelter of the barn with her camera.

"If you have nothing useful to say, then zip it would you, Bon," I remembered him calling out as he unsuccessfully tried to herd the sheep.

After an hour of going around in circles, Neville came to find us and when he did, a look of amusement spread across his face.

"You have got to be kidding," he laughed, watching as my father again ran around in a circle, narrowly missing the sheep.

"We tried to explain to him," my mother said as she reached for her camera rested on a timber ledge.

"Clearly, only one of us has the farmer genes," Graeme muttered. "Finny, would you mind getting me the whistle?"

I nodded, running out into the rain to get the whistle

from dad much to his reluctance. All it took from Graeme were four clear and articulate whistles before the dogs penned the sheep safely inside.

My father said not a word as he walked past us all in hysterics, muddied to the knees and fatigued. Later that night the sheep safely gave birth to which Graeme jokingly called Spud after his nickname for my father.

"I would have got the sheep in the end, you know," he said with a subtle smirk on his lips.

"I'm sure you would have," I laughed, turning the page.

I could see what Dr Wells meant. The past few days, I struggled emotionally with the idea that I was losing him. His memories were now more in the past than they were in the present. His voice remained inaudible mostly, with his chest still heavy from the lingering infection he was recovering from. With each page we turned, I could see the memory reel light up in his eyes. Each time he smiled, a faint glimmer of hope all was not lost circulated through me.

"Can we do this again?" he whispered as he placed his hands over my own.

"Of course, da. I would like that."

Back at my apartment that evening, despite the joy I experienced seeing my father's pleasure, my heart was heavy. Seeing the images, not only of my mother, but Lyall too, disturbed something within me.

I mused over those thoughts as I stood in my kitchen pan frying a steak. The sun was going down, illuminating an orange glow over the varnished timber floors. My mother thought me and my father daft when he insisted I purchase this place for 100k four years ago. It was now double that, given the work my father, and I put into the place. It was a bittersweet feeling, knowing that when he passed, I would likely have to sell. I had no purpose in coming back to Aberdeen when he was gone. It didn't feel right to rent it out either, given the horror stories I was told by others.

I sat myself at the breakfast bar, staring at the exposed rafters overhead. I brought no one back there and yet when my mother and I had painted those very rafters in an off shade of white, she jokingly passed a comment that eventually she hoped she would get an invitation when I met someone to have dinner.

I would hold on to it a little while, I thought to myself as I cut my steak. It was now mortgage free from the inheritance I gained from my mother, so it cost me very little. After I finished my dinner, I felt exhausted, yet my mind was racing a million miles an hour, unable to switch off. In an attempt to shake my thoughts, I slipped into the shower and my thoughts drifted to Ainsley. I visualised her easy smile and the way she laughed, and the memory caused my heart to quicken.

Perhaps Blair had been right. There was another force at work; something I was trying to deny. She became more attractive to me the more time I spent with her, and I thought about her more than I cared to admit. I stared at my reflection as I stepped out of the shower, knowing something had to give. When my father passed, I would be two hours south and nothing would be as it was then. She wasn't ready for that kind of commitment, neither was I, not yet anyway.

Then again, I heard a voice inside my whisper. Maybe I was.

Blame

Several days after the trip to Nairn, my father came down with a nasty bronchial infection and I found myself riddled with guilt, given I knew our escapade was likely to blame. Ainsley did her best to reason with me given my father wasn't the only one on his ward that came down with the infection, but I couldn't help myself but questioning whether my stupidity caused it.

Sitting up right, my father stared blankly out the window, his breath rattled and shallow. The very little colouring he had became non-existent; his skin pale and dry.

"Is he okay within himself?" I questioned Ainsley as she took his vitals.

"He hasn't said a word today," she replied, glancing at me briefly as she recorded his blood pressure.

I leaned back in my chair, observing her demeanour. She seemed unusually distant; each reply to my questions feeling forced.

"Is something wrong?"

She shook her head, not saying a word, ignoring the question.

"Ainsley..."

"Forget it." She replied hastily, her eyes diverting

everywhere but towards mine.

"Forget what? I am not a mind reader."

"Just drop it Finn," she snapped, noting the time and disappearing into the hallway.

After a short visit with Dad, I made my way to Blair's to help him replace some spouting on his parents' house. His father became increasingly unwell, his lungs showing the signs of the five-decade long infatuation with cigarettes. Neither of us had any knowledge of what we were doing but assumed it couldn't be hard. I mean, how hard could it be?

"How is the redhead?" Blair asked as he pulled the spouting off the back of his father's truck.

I replied with a shrug. "She is in a mood about something this morning."

"Well, Finny, I ain't surprised. You guys are spending a lot of time together."

"We are just friends," I replied defiantly.

"Does she know that?"

I hesitated. It was something we brought up in conversation, but she never directly questioned me on the matter.

"Given your silence, I assume not." Blair smirked as he pulled out a measuring tape from the cab on his father's truck.

"It has come up in conversation. It's not as if we haven't discussed it at all."

"There is a difference between conversation and actually discussing things you know."

"Since when were you an expert?"

Blair laughed, his head tilted back. "I never claimed to be. I like her Finn. She seems like a nice lass."

"She is."

"So why the reluctance?"

"I am in Edinburgh. She is here. It would never work."

The distance was a lie, but it seemed easier to falsify a reason from it than it would be to explain otherwise. I had my reasons – reasons in which I didn't expect Blair or Ainsley to understand. Maybe I thought I would tell her about those things. Or maybe I wouldn't? The details seemed irrelevant since I had decided we would never work. Many had told me that what happened in childhood should not define me. The thing is, how could it not? Blair, despite knowing me most of my life knew absolutely nothing about it. No one did.

"Oh c'mon Finn, it's not far. Dinnae be so glaikit – dae something!"

I shook my head, "Wheesht! It's not happening."

Blair surrendered his quest for answers, not bringing it up again until later that evening when we met with Colin and a few other friends at a bar in the city. I briefly went back to visit Dad, but he was fast asleep and Ainsley had finished her shift earlier on in the afternoon.

After we all had a few too many pints and several rowdy rounds of playing pool, Blair slapped me firmly in the back. "Why don't you see if she wants to come down? Everyone else's lasses are here."

"She isn't my lass," I said with a laugh, sinking the last of my pint.

"She is the closest thing to one."

Against my better judgement, I invited Ainsley, and she arrived a short time later. As she walked in wearing a mustard trench coat and short black dress underneath, I knew all eyes were on her. Colin's fiancée, Amy, stared in my direction, holding her glass centimetres from her lips, her eyes wide with curiosity. Michelle, who had just brought back refilled pints, went abnormally silent.

"They are watching us," Ainsley whispered in my ear as she gave me a brief, distant hug.

"Of course they are. They really aren't the vultures they seem right now," I said with a laugh as I released her.

"Finn –" Ainsley tried to tell me something, but Michelle interrupted us as she brought over a full pint of beer for Ainsley.

"Ainsley right? Hi, I'm Blair's partner and that's Amy." She pointed over to the slim brunette seated in a booth to the left, who gave her a hesitant but friendly wave.

"Hi," Ainsley said, her voice flustered as she panned the bar.

"Come with me," Michelle said, leading her towards Amy. "You don't want to hang out with those idiots."

Throughout the night Ainsley danced, sang and smiled, fitting in as if she had been part of our crew for years, but something bothered me. I could sense she was still harbouring the secret of her evident hostility from earlier as she did her best to smile, but I found her several times glancing in my direction, her face downcast.

"I really like her, Finn," Colin said as I accompanied him outside for a fag.

I hadn't seen Colin since my mother had passed. In the dimly lit courtyard, I studied the wrinkles appearing around the corners of his eyes, realising just how much he had aged. "Are ye sleeping? Looking old there," I joked, changing the subject.

"Kids, I tell ye Finn, one is more than enough."

Even though Amy and Colin had recently got engaged, they had four children all under six years. Twin boys Sam and Emmet, Suzie, and their youngest, another wee boy they named after Colin's father, William.

"So not four then?"

"Well, I wouldn't say it is for the faint hearted." He replied, stubbing his fag into the ash tray. "Back to this Ainsley."

"Nay, don't do it man. Blair already beat ye to it."

Colin looked at me directly in the eye, as if he was trying to read my thoughts. "I see the way she looks at ye, Finn. If you just messin', it's time to front up. It would be cruel to let it continue."

There was a silence when I stared at the brazier in the far left corner, my liquor confidence waning. What did Ainsley and I have to do anything with anyone else?

"Hows ye da?" Colin finally said in response to my silence, pulling himself another fag from his pocket.

"Those things will kill ye," I said, watching as he set

the end alight.

"Probably. Here for a good time, not a long time."

"Da, he ain't good. Reckon he is close."

"Shit, I'm sorry. Didn't realise it was that bad."

I paused as I glanced back inside at Ainsley, noticing she was looking directly at me. When my gaze met hers, she looked away. Something was off and I knew I needed to talk to her. I tried to wrap my head around why everyone seemed convinced Ainsley and I had become a thing. It was not something we had discussed other than the vague conversation at the summit the day before.

"Aye, life right? It's short."

"Ye right there. Even so, it must be rough."

I nodded in reply, still keeping my eyes on Ainsley.

"No question who ye are looking at" Colin said with a laugh as he exhaled the smoke from his lungs.

"She is Irish, right?"

"Aye."

"Well, she is good for you."

"There is nothing going on."

Colin glanced over towards Ainsley, Michelle, and Amy as they sat at the bar, all in a fit of laughter.

"If you don't see Finn, you are more of an asshole than I thought." He gave me a heavy slap on the back, and we made our way inside.

Ainsley saw me making my way inside and glared at me, signalling for me to come to her. "What's wrong?" I whispered as I nudged myself closer to her.

She looked to her feet, placing her empty glass on the table. "Finn, can we talk? Outside?"

We made our way to the small smoko courtyard outside where Colin and I had just come from. She took a deep breath, unable to look directly in the eye and for a moment we stood in an awkward silence against the backdrop of the brazier crackling.

"Finn, I can't do this anymore," she finally said, biting her lip several times.

I stared at her, confused as she does her best attempt to fixate on the flames of the brazier.

"Do what?"

"This," she said, gesturing with her hands back and forth between us.

"It's not professional. It shouldn't be happening. So we need to keep it simply that – professional."

"Ainsley…"

She shook her head. "Finn, I'm sorry this should never have happened. It is against conduct and I need my job. I love my job."

"So, wait, you can't be friends with people when their parents are under your care?"

She finally caught my gaze and I could see her eyes were watery. "Finn, please don't make me do this."

"Do what? I'm the one who is confused here."

"I've crossed a line. I don't expect you to understand."

"Crossed a line, how?"

She shook her head. For the first time, she seemed to question what she was saying, and her lip quivered. When she spoke again, her voice trembled. "Please, Finn, don't."

"Don't what?"

"Please don't make me do this."

I looked at her, feeling frustrated, intoxicated, and confused, unable to decipher what was happening. "Do what exactly? Please spell it out for me because I have no idea what is going on here?"

Her answer was slow in coming. "I no longer see you as a friend and that is the problem."

I stood frozen as I stared in her eyes, unable to vocalise a response. Ever since the first dinner, I had thought about her with greater frequency. They were vague thoughts, edged with curiosity and the blind knowledge that I enjoyed her company. I had dated no one other than Brianna. All other relationships I had simply existed in my bedroom's four walls, nothing more. While I had my reasons behind not seeking companionship, I also had little time to go out. I had always thrown myself into my career, working long hours and months away on deployment. Yes, it was sometimes hard, and yes, sometimes I was lonely. I could never be what she needed me to be. I made a choice long ago.

"Ainsley, I –"

"Finn," she interrupted as she raised her hand to her face. "I don't expect you to say anything. I know how this goes and I'm fine. I just wanted you to know that we can't do this anymore."

All I could do was nod before she politely excused herself and I watched her walk away. Every fibre of me was aching to go after her, but I found myself stuck, unsure of what the right and wrong thing was to do. In my anger, fuelled not only by the situation but by blood alcohol level, I picked up Ainsley's glass, smashing it to the ground. A shard, embedded in my knuckle, caused a fast-flowing bloodied wound and my night came to an abrupt end.

When I arrived to see Dad the following day, his health had deteriorated even further, with Ainsley suggesting that they may have to move him to the hospital. She did her best to act professional, but you could cut the tension filled air with a knife. Dad eventually came right after a week, but he was getting worse. His moments of lucidity became further and further apart. He became so thin that his face, with his last bout of illness, was becoming barely recognisable. I had promised my mother that I would stick by his side no matter how ugly and how hard it became, but it became overwhelmingly hard.

The change in mine and Ainsley's relationship triggered a grief I never expected I would feel. We hadn't known each other long, but it was in the absence of that very relationship that I longed for the comfort it had once given me. She would deliberately excuse herself with every visit and I found myself desperate just to hear her laugh again; longing to hear her voice. When our relationship changed, so did my visits, and not just because of my father's ailing health.

Whisky

Two weeks passed and my father had fallen into a state of rapid decline. His chest infection resulted in a week-long stay in hospital and while he eventually recovered, it seemed to have taken a toll of its own. Nobody could give me answers why it seemed like a light switch had gone off and taking his health with it. Ainsley did her best to keep her distance, but it was hard. Her avoidance didn't go unnoticed, clear when the practice manager of the clinic asked to speak with me, voicing concerns from other staff regarding her hostility towards me.

The morning she requested to see me, I was in foul spirits, exhausted from worrying whether or not my father was on his last stretch. I wasn't in the mood for entertaining gossip but wasn't convinced my lying abilities would be half as good as I thought they were.

"Did something happen?" she questioned, taking a sip of her coffee.

I stared at her for a moment, unsure of how to reply in a convincing manner. Her eyes were nearly black with an unusual intensity about them. She looked as if she had walked around the sun a few times and could sniff out a lie, which did nothing to ease my nervousness.

"Not at all," I replied, doing my best to sound believable.

"I talked it over with our charge nurse and we are looking at our staffing to move her to another patient."

"No," I said abruptly, which caused her to look at me with a confused glare.

"Sorry, I mean, everything is well. My father likes her, I like her. I assume she has things going on in her private life."

There was a moment's silence and I could feel her eyes on me. I did my best to look over her shoulder, fixated on a picture of two white swans in the far corner.

"Okay, if you are happy then we will leave as is."

I felt a lump in my throat as I left her office, questioning if my ability to lie had been successful. I am sure she could tell from my off-pitch and rushed replies to her questions something was amiss even if she couldn't pinpoint exactly what.

I made my way down the hallway. I could see Ainsley grabbing sheets from a linen trolley three rooms down from Dad's room. She glanced at me briefly before turning her attention back to what she was doing.

"Ainsley, wait," I called out to her as I quickened my step.

"Yes?" she questioned, her voice sounding irritated as she refused to look at me.

I held my breath, doing a quick check behind me for any incoming unwanted attention.

"Look, can't we just go back to how it was?" I paused, hearing the exit door swing, and another nurse made her way past us, giving us both a genuine smile. Once she was out of audible range, we continued.

"I had a meeting."

"With who?" Ainsley questioned as she continued to search the trolley.

"I can't remember her name. Tall lady, dark shoulder length hair. She is the practice manager, I believe."

"Sue?" Her voice suddenly became alarmed.

"Must have been. Anyway..." I continued before Ainsley abruptly interrupted me in panic. "She –"

"Wait, why?" she queried as she bent down to grab a pillowcase from the second shelf of the trolley. "Because of me?"

"She was asking me if I had concerns about the care you are giving Dad as some nurses had sensed that things were off."

"And do you?" her voice sounded agitated and I

could sense she was nervous.

"Do I what?" I questioned as I stared at her.

"Have concerns?"

"Of course, I don't. Why would you even think that?"

After a moment of silence passed with us both staring at each other in the barren hallway, Ainsley took a deep breath and ended the awkwardness with an excuse to leave. "I have to go Finn," She paused. "Your dad isn't too great today, just a word of warning."

I nodded in reply and continued on down to my father's room.

Ainsley was right. When I saw my father lying on his side on his bed for a brief second, I had lost him. His frail body was curled into a near fetal position as he took several loud, laboured breaths.

"Hi, da," I whispered, my voice trembling as I took a seat next to him.

He didn't even look up to acknowledge me, instead fixed his view on the skirting on the wall. His words sounded inebriated, slurred and unrecognisable. I sat down in the lone chair as I had so many times before, only this time I was convinced it would be the last time I would be doing that in his presence. Death had never scared me. Even on my three deployments, when I knew the possibility was heightened, it wasn't something I had ever given much thought. The thought of losing my father, however, scared me.

I moved myself closer and watched as he did a weakened shuffle in his bed, his eyes fluttering.

I leaned closer to his bed, squeezing his hand.

"Hey, da, I'm here. Can you hear me?"

He turned his head, only a little, but as much as he could to look at me.

"It's me, Finn. Ye okay in there?"

He blinked slowly, his breathing rattled. "Fin... n."

"Aye da, it's me. Ye feeling poorly?"

I tried to inject humour into the situation, but it was becoming emotionally unattainable and tears ran down my face.

I felt him squeeze my hand.

"I... need... care..."

"You are da," I said. "They're taking good care of you."

"Where... is... she..."

Each word croaked out between ragged breaths.

"Where is who, da?" I questioned as I leaned closer to hear his words clearer.

"Bonnie..."

I looked away in an effort to console myself, unsure how to answer. "Da, it's Finn, Mum she couldn't come." As I said it, I wondered if in his mind he remotely believed it.

"Sick."

He seemed abnormally delirious, which only exaggerated my concern that he was fast approaching his final hour.

"You'll be okay," I lied. "And tomorrow we can watch the boats."

"To...mo... rrow?"

I squeezed his hand again, hating his confusion, hating that he didn't know what had happened to him or who he was anymore. "Aye, we will go tomorrow and we can watch the boats. How does that sound?"

There was a pause in his words as he took several deepened wheezy breaths.

"Where.... is... Lyall?" He finally spoke and my heart sunk.

I didn't have the heart to remind him about Lyall; its significance seemed vastly unimportant, given his condition. "You'll see him soon," I promised. "And ma, you will see her soon." I wiped a tear from my cheek, taking a deep breath.

"Go... away."

I froze, wondering if I'd heard him right. If he was attempting some kind of joke, it was one that would be out of character for him. "It's okay, I'm here," I repeated.

"Finn... go." He repeated, this time more stern.

"I'm not leaving you," I replied, squeezing his hand again, convinced it was just his confused mind talking and not his wishes. "I'm staying right here. His expression softened.

"Finn... You... came..."

"Of course, I came."

"Now go..."

"No," I said. "I'm going to stay right here."

"Please," he whispered before he closed his eyes and weakly rolled himself away from me, facing the window.

"Da, don't be like this," I murmured, wiping my wet cheeks on my sleeve.

He said nothing in reply, only tilting his head slightly to the left as if to catch me in his peripherals. I sat for a while, watching the rise and fall of his chest with each deep rasped breath. I wasn't ready to lose him; the thought terrified me. I needed more time. He couldn't do this to me, not today.

Sometime later, Ainsley gently knocked on the door. "How is he?"

"You can come in," I said as I glanced at her, sensing her reluctance.

She paused, looking at me before looking at him. "Are you sure?"

"Yes, of course, I'm sure." I retorted, wiping my face again.

She hesitantly stepped inside, closing the door gently behind her. "He isn't very well, is he?" she replied solemnly, as she walked herself around to the opposite side of the bed, staring at his monitor.

"I mean, his stats are okay for now. His oxygen and pulse are good, but he sounds quite poor. I'm sorry Finn," she said, her gaze lowered.

"Is this it? Is this how he will go out?" I asked her, as if she could give me the answer. I looked at her in panic, but she refused to meet my gaze.

"Finn, I..." she shook her head twice and wrapped a cuff around his thin arms to check his blood pressure. "Sometimes they have days like this and then their health rebounds."

I knew she was trying to sugar-coat it, given her words didn't carry the same genuineness as they usually did.

"Ainsley, I'm not asking you for a generic answer. I think we passed generic answers a long time ago."

She looked to her feet, drawing a deep, shaky breath. "Finn, I think he is very close. But I don't have the answer to that."

I could tell the news was one she didn't want to

give me. In her eyes, I saw sadness, one I had never seen before. For a moment, I studied her, watching as he wiped a tear from her sleeve.

"I'm sorry I –"

"Finn, it's okay," she replied, giving me a fleeting glance before coaxing my father to lie on his back before she gently tucked him into bed.

"Ainsley, look I just, I want things to go back to normal. I could really use a friend."

"I'm sorry I complicated things. None of this should have ever happened. I should never have invited you to dinner. I should-."

"Stop." I shook my head. "I am glad you did."

She smiled at me softly as she took my father's pulse.

"I will stay with him tonight and will ring you if things go really downhill."

"I hope they don't," I replied, watching as he stared at the ceiling, still taking rapid, heaved breaths.

"I hope so too Finn, I promise I will ring you if I fear it is coming."

"Thank you."

That evening, I stayed at home and not at my apartment. It was odd being at the house. It felt empty without my father and as I wandered the rooms, which were fast becoming coated in dust, the feeling of loss deepened. It had the same cluttered atmosphere as the house I had always known, but it felt as if its heart was missing. As I made my way up the stairs I stopped at the landing, resting my eyes on a picture of us three the Christmas before my mother died. With all the energy that I had dedicated to my father, I felt I was losing her. The ability to remember her face, the way she laughed, and the way she smiled. I felt I was forgetting. I realised when I saw her, dressed in jeans and a white button-down shirt, she smiled back at me with her eyes creased in the corners even if I thought I was, I never would.

"There ye are, ma," I smiled to myself. "I hope you haven't met a toyboy yet because da, he is coming for you. He is going to be coming for you real soon." My mother had always joked towards the end of her battle that she was going to trade up behind the pearly gates as she knew it wound my father up like a tight spring.

My bedroom at home had not been updated since I was a teenager, still decorated with faded KISS Posters and a seductive picture of Carmen Electra bent over a Ford Mustang. As I climbed into the sheets, sheets I hadn't slept in years, I felt a sudden wave of calm spread through my body. I never thought in my thirties I would find solace in my time capsule bedroom of a previous life. Yet there I was, with the faint background hum of the motorway; I took a sip of my father's whisky, scared I may never see him alive again.

The Surge

My father made it through the night and the following morning it was as if he was a different person.

Of all the things people had told me over the duration of Dad's illness, I wished someone had told me more about the surge. The day Dad died I arrived to see him sitting upright in bed, deep in conversation with Ainsley as she sat next to him, focusing attentively as if yesterday hadn't happened.

After weeks of barely hearing his voice as he welcomed me into his room with his weakened raspy voice, it sent a shiver up my spine. I had become lost in my world of hopelessly trying to connect with him through his soft mumbling and erratic noises the past two weeks, that I couldn't contain my emotion in my confusion.

Ainsley had briefly touched on the surge she experienced with her own mother and even though it didn't register immediately, once I connected the dots, I couldn't evade the feeling of needing to run away.

"I'm sorry," I said, glancing at Ainsley in a state

of panic before excusing myself into the hallway.

"Finn, are you okay?" I hear Ainsley's voice a short time later as she popped her head out of dad's room.

I couldn't look at her without feeling I was going to break in two, so I kept my gaze firmly fixed on the clock on the wall in front of me. For a moment, I got lost in the tranquil sound of it ticking, watching as the hands delicately shudder with each passing second.

"Finn..."

Ainsley calling my name again, abruptly ended the tranquillity. I shook my head, still unable to look at her, feeling the burn of tears well in my eyes.

"Finn, look at me!"

I glanced at her briefly before the anger pursed on my lips escaped. "What the fuck is that?" I stammered, gesturing in my father's direction. "Tell me what the fuck is that!"

I knew she wanted to tell me, but she couldn't. As I briefly glanced at her face, I could see it written in her sympathetic down cast stare, all I needed to know.

"Finn, look, I..." She broke from my gaze momentarily, running her hand over her cheek.

"I can't do this," I said, my voice trembling.

"He needs you."

"And you think I don't need him?" I paused, staring at her in utter desperation. "I'm not ready, Ainsley. I can't…"

Still standing in the doorway, she glanced over her shoulder back at Dad. "I don't know how long he's got Finn, but all I know is right here, right now, he needs you. He is here, and he needs you."

How did she expect me to pretend I was okay when I felt every piece of me was crumbling?

"I know, Finn, this is hard, but do you know what is even harder? If you choose to walk away, unable to deal with this and losing this chance; a chance you may never get again."

I nodded, unable to form any words before reluctantly making my way back into the room where Dad was staring out the window, talking about how he wanted to go to the beach.

"Finn, you can do this," Ainsley whispered to me as I walked past her, briefly catching her eye.

I let out a deep sigh and walked over to the right side of the bed. "So where would you like to go today, da?"

"Aye, Finny," he said cheerfully. "Look at the weather!"

"Beauty, ain't it?" I mumbled, trying to hold back my emotions.

"I think we should take ye Ma to the beach."

I could feel Ainsley watching me as I became stuck, unsure of how to answer his request.

"Might just have to be you two today. I think she is working now," Ainsley interrupted, shooting me a smile.

"That's a shame, but perhaps she can come tomorrow?"

"Aye Dad, perhaps she can."

We got Dad organised, and I thanked Ainsley before Dad and I headed out the door.

"Finn, you can do this. Just remember that."

I nodded in response, trying to convince myself she was right.

We headed out into the city and Dad confessed to me he wanted to buy some new winter clothes. Part of me knew it would be wasted money, but it provided a distraction from the reality I knew we faced. I watched him smiling as he picked out a bunch of new plaid shirts. I could do nothing to save myself from escaping the pain that felt heavy in my heart. It was easy, as I shut my eyes briefly to convince myself somehow Dad recovered or at least improved and that the months we faced were all a nightmare that we had finally woken up from. I knew he was dying. I knew this as it was exactly what Ainsley described, but that day my mind longed to feel otherwise.

"Should we go to a hole in the wall? Finny, I'm

feeling knackered," he said after we paid for his new shirts.

"Sounds like a good plan," I said, grabbing the bags from the counter, wheeling him outside.

I helped Dad into the car and knew exactly where I was going to take him. When I came of age, we would often go to a small hole in the wall close to home where we could see the ships coming into the berth. Dad had always cherished the sea, and once you started him on the topic, it would be hard to make him stop. It became frustrating at times and Mum once confessed to me she speculated he was on the Asperger's spectrum since he would fixate on it. Asperger's or not, I was happy for him to talk about the sea because I was just grateful for the first time in a long time to hear his voice.

The watering hole was barren minus two elderly gentlemen deep in discussion in the far-right corner when we arrived.

"Finn, I haven't seen you in donkey days," Fran the barmaid said as she shot Dad a smile.

"Aye, it has been a while," I said in response, helping Dad into our usual seat.

"How is he?" she asked, bringing over two pints.

"He is doing good, aren't ya, Da?"

Dad nodded, giving Fran a wide smile tinged with uncertainty.

"Tell ya what, how about I put on one of your

favourite songs?" Fran winked at Dad before making her way over to the duke box.

Fran had known my father since he was a boy, as they grew up in the same neighbourhood. That day, he seemed unable to connect the source of her familiarity.

"Lovely lady that one is," he said weakly, taking a sip of his pint glancing out the window.

I observed Fran study the jukebox, deep in thought, before suddenly *Annie Laurie* by the Corries blasted from the speakers.

"I haven't heard this song for years," Dad said with a chuckle.

I couldn't help but smile as Fran chose the song that Dad would always jokingly sing to my mother. I dropped my gaze, running my finger over the rim of the glass, remembering a time when I had come home early from a party to find them both dancing in our lounge, unaware of my presence.

"You are absurd." I remember hearing my mother snort as he whisked her around.

"Maxwelton braes are Bonnie, where early fa's the dew." Dad laughed in response, to her delight.

I remember watching them, intoxicated by their devotion to each other. Nobody seemed to understand my father like she did, and nobody seemed to help Mum relax as he could.

"Your Ma, she loves this song," Dad said, breaking my thoughts.

"Does she now? I think she despises it, actually."

"She may tell ye that Finny, but she secretly loves it."

"Aye, I think you are wrong there," I said, laughing as I took another sip of my pint while Dad stared at me with a sly grin spread across his face.

Once we finished our pints, I ordered us some hot chips, and we made our way out to the water's edge to observe the boats come in.

Dad was busy staring out at the fishing trawlers coming into the port, fending seagulls away from his uneaten hot chips, when my phone rang from an unknown number. I paused, staring at the screen in hesitation as usually a restricted number would be from work, but I was on leave.

"Ello?" I answered.

"Finn, it's Colin," I heard Colin's voice quietly from the other end of the line. I felt something was amiss. Colin was always someone you could hear well before you could see him with his thick northern accent. His quietness startled me.

"Ai, Colin how are ya?"

Colin was a friend of mine I had not seen in years. Not through choice. Our lives had drifted apart where he was based down in Manchester with his family and the rest of us spread out between Edinburgh and home.

There was a pause before Colin cleared his throat. "Not great, Finn," he said, leaving me feeling uneasy given his solemn tone. "I just got a phone call from Blair's family. Blair, he... Well, he tried to take his own life last night."

My heart sank. What was he talking about when I had just spoken to Blair a day or two back and he, on all accounts, seemed fine?

I glanced over at Dad, who was still trying to fend off the gulls, lost in a babble of his slurred words as he continued to watch the activity in the port.

"Nay, I was just speaking to him the other day, ye dafty" I said, baffled, questioning if he was pranking me or not.

When he didn't laugh, I had all I needed to know.

"Finny, I ain't joking, mate. Promise ye."

There was a period of silence and my mind tried to digest what Colin had just told me, and I could hear Colin murmur something to someone in the background. "I'm heading up there soon. Are you up visiting the old man?"

"Ye, I am. I won't be able to go down there until the weekend at least."

"Aye, he will understand. I'll give you a ring when I get some updates. Ye?"

"Aye, cheers."

I slid my phone in the pocket of my jeans, trying to process the shock, and made my way over to Dad, who was still having battles with one lone, courageous seagull. My head was a mess, perplexed by the conversation that had just transpired.

"Everything all right there?" he turned to me, puzzled by my expression. "Spit it out!"

I let out a long exhale, grasping the railing with my hands. "Dad, do you remember Blair?"

"The redhead that never shuts up?"

I couldn't control my laughter at his bluntness, even if it was the first time he had been accurate in quite some time. Blair had a mop of thick red hair and could talk about the back legs of a donkey. It was what would become part of a puzzling feature for me about his actions and a cause for a great deal of questioning. I just never saw that side of him, a side that would even assimilate such a choice. He had, as of late after the breakup of his six-year relationship, become far too indulgent of the local pub and given I had been on leave for the last three weeks trying to get Dad sorted, maybe I had missed something.

"That's the one, Dad" I said, staring out towards the stormy foaming sea.

"Aye, I remember. Pleasant lad, that one," Dad said as changed his gaze to the sea with me.

"So, what happened? Is he all right?"

I took a deep breath, knowing Dad would probably not recall the news tomorrow. "Well Dad, he…" I paused, watching the sea crash into the seawall. "He, Dad, he tried to kill himself."

There was a silence as we both examined the waves coming in before Dad patted me on the back. "Finny, I am going to tell you something I don't think I have ever told no one. Come to think of it, I don't even think I ever told ye mother." He paused his train of thought as a couple walked past us, holding hands in their own world of conversation. "I tried once."

I turned and faced him, uncertain of what to say as he kept his gaze firmly out to sea.

"It was after we lost your brother." His voice trembled as he paused, taking a deep breath. "I blamed myself so much, Finny. I had been checking out the game having a few beers while your mother was at work on the night shift, and you were tucked up in bed asleep. I questioned myself for months after it happened whether maybe I had not checked him enough that night. Did I place him down on his back? Did I miss any noises that could have alerted me that something was amiss? One day it all just got too much, and I was going to do it. I was at the point, and I was just going to jump. I knew it would be near instantaneous and that the current would more than likely take me out so that your mum wouldn't have to deal with seeing it. The thing is Finny, I saw no other option, but I couldn't go through with it. I was right there, ready to meet my end and I just…

Well, I couldn't do it."

"Well, I'm glad you didn't, Dad," I whispered, staring as he wiped a tear from his eye.

"It still sometimes gets me, Finn, that I would have even considered doing that to both of you. It stopped me, you see; thinking of you, your mother, the life we had, and I just realised it would have been a mistake." He glanced at me with a pained expression, one I had never seen before. "Ye mate, Blair, he would've seen no option. He would have had his reasons and ultimately he would have felt no other way out."

"He always seems so happy," I said quietly, fidgeting with my thumb.

"Finny, often the happiest people you see are the loneliest and the most depressed. People really are not that smart. It is easy to fool people into thinking you are fine when inside you are anything but." He paused again, briefly glancing at me before diverting his attention back to the port. "Are you going to see him?"

"Aye, maybe on the weekend," I replied.

He nodded as he studied my face. "Are you going to be okay?"

I felt I would be, but I was full of questions. He had been the brother I never got the chance to have, and I didn't want to lose him, too.

"I am always here for you, Finny, if you need me.

I realise I am slowly losing my marbles, but I will always do my best." He looked at me intensively with his blue eyes that were looking cloudy, coated in a fine grey film. "I mean it Finn."

"I know, Dad," I said as I planted three gentle pats on his back before I wheeled him back to the car.

Driving Dad back to the care home was met with silence. I guess we were both deep in reflection. Me about what could be Blair's reasons for doing what he did and Dad, well, I was seeing signs he was losing the grips of his consciousness.

Before I helped him out of the car, I turned to face him as he tried to figure out where he was.

"Da, I need to tell you something. I love you and I... I am so grateful."

"Finn?" he asked. "Where are we?"

I realised I had lost him and the next fifteen minutes would be difficult.

It was always difficult parting with Dad when he became distressed at the realisation he now lived in a care facility and not in the home we once all shared.

"Finny, Finny, where are you going?" he panicked as I handed him over to his nurses, unable to stop the tears flowing like a river down my face.

I hated walking away, even though time had taught me it was all I could do. Initially, I used to stay and do my best to soothe him, but it only made things worse.

"Finny, who are these people?" he called out, panicked as they held him back.

"Finny," he yelled again, desperately trying to fend off the firm grip of his nurses. He sounded terrified, and rightly so, as he did not recognise who they were.

I closed my eyes as I reached the exit doors, wanting to look back, but I couldn't. If he was to die as Ainsley warned me he might, I didn't want his face as he watched me walk away to be my last memory.

"Dad, I love you. I love you so much," I whispered, pausing with my hands clasped around the exit door handle.

At least for that day, Dad shared with me a part of him I had never seen before and a part of me I knew I would never see again.

The Final Goodbye

On my second tour in Iraq, seated playing cards with Blair and another colleague James, I would learn something I would never forget. James, who was a scrawny potty mouthed lad from a village on the outskirts of Glasgow, relayed that evening to Blair and I how he had dreamt on the night his father had passed. We both laughed given we had all experienced some rather unsavoury dreams, fuelled by fatigue and events of the times. Reality struck the following day. He found out his dream wasn't a dream at all and his father had died in the night after a suspected heart attack. It was something that intrigued me, and I dedicated hours of research in my spare time. Blair considered the idea ludicrous, but for me, it was something that stayed with me.

The night my mother passed, something awoke me shortly after one in the morning feeling as if someone stroked my face. Since returning from Iraq, I always slept with two LED lights on, giving me enough illumination to establish my surroundings quickly. I panned my room in a daze, confused, before falling back asleep. The following morning, I remember touching my face. The sensation still lingered on my cheeks, and then the phone rang.

Perhaps it was superstitious, but the night my father died, I could not shake the restless stir within my soul.

There was a sense something was not quite right, but I was unable to pinpoint what. I would doze off only to wake again, confused by why I was restless. At the time, I didn't recognise that it was happening again and shrugged it off that maybe I had become overtired. My experience overseas had taught me the less I slept, the harder it became to sleep, so naturally it was my first thought.

Shortly after three in the morning, I stared at the ceiling, reflecting on what Dad had said after hearing about Blair. What remained uncertain to me was whether his words were the dementia talking or whether there was truth laced in his words. Haunted by what he had confessed, I fixated on every word.

If that had been true, had my mother speculated about it?

I let out a groan, hearing the rattle of the train tracks in the distance. My father had been so present that day, even if his mobility wasn't as it used to be. For the first time in months, I felt I had seen him, really seen him, and not just the shell of the man I once knew.

Alone with my thoughts, I must have eventually drifted off, for I was awoken some time later by my phone ringing loudly from my bedside table.

"Who the fuck is ringing me at this hour" I mumbled, rummaging for my phone with closed eyes. Once I felt the familiar coolness in my grasp, I opened my eyes. In my half-asleep state, I could not compute the number flashing in my blurred vision.

"Hello, Finn speaking," I grumbled, blinking twice to wake my eyes from their slumber.

"Finn" I heard Ainsley's voice sniff from the other end of the line and I instantly jolted upright.

"What is wrong?"

There was a long pause, and suddenly I realized. Why else would she be ringing me at four in the morning.

"No, no. Please don't tell me." I begged, beginning to cry.

"Finn, I'm sorry."

"No, please Ainsley, I need more time."

After a moment's silence, I hear Ainsley sniff. "You can come down and see him if you like. Finn, it was fast. I was with him when it happened. I assure you, it was peaceful."

I could hear her sob at the end of her last sentence, which only exacerbated my own restrained sobs.

I struggled to find any words, instead picking up my pillow and screaming into it uncontrollably.

Once I was able to compose myself, I picked up my phone again.

"I'm coming down now," I whispered, my tone off pitch.

"I'll meet you in the lobby if you message me when you are here," she replied quietly before hanging up.

The five-minute drive to the facility felt like hours. In my dazed, confused state I felt I was on autopilot watching myself in third person. When I arrived, as I made my way up to the brightly lit lobby, I could see Ainsley standing waiting for me as if she knew I would instinctively forget to message her in my shock.

"I'm not ready," I repeated over and over in shock as she took me into her arms, engulfing me in the perfumed scent of her hair.

"When you are ready, we will go, okay?"

How was I ever meant to be ready?

"Finn, I promise you it happened fast, and I held his hand."

"Was he okay?" I questioned as I pulled back from her. She had done her best to wipe her face, but I could see black smeared mascara lines run down her cheek.

She squeezed my hand tenderly with a soft nod. "He was okay, and most importantly, he was not alone."

"Okay," I whispered, exhaling loudly, which trailed with several tremors. "I'm ready."

"Are you sure? Take as much time as you need."

"No, I'm okay. I'm ready," I reply, drying my cheeks with my sleeve.

We made the trip to his room in silence, pausing as we reached the door. I felt my heart racing, unsure of what to expect on the other side of the door.

"I'll be right here," Ainsley said, as she glanced at some other nurses observing me from their station.

I took a deep breath before I entered the room, thanking her for her support. Instead of the continuous beep of his heart monitor, the room lay silent with Dad laying marginally inclined with his arms placed over his chest. I stood at the foot of his bed, studying him in his peaceful slumber. I was frozen, unable to move.

"Dad, sorry I couldn't be here. I..." I shook my head, clutching the cool metal footer of the bed. "I know you can't hear me. I... Dad... I... I had so much more I wished to say to you."

I strolled over to the right-hand side of the bed, lowering myself into the seat next to him, staring at his hands placed across his chest. I was hesitant to grab them, unsure of the warmth they would reciprocate.

When my mother passed, I had been down in Edinburgh, which was two and a half hours south. Dad called me the following morning and by the time I got there, she was already at the morgue.

Ainsley gently tapped on the door to alert me to her presence.

I glanced at her, unsure of what to say.

"He won't be cold," she stated, as if she could read my startled expression.

"Wait." I looked at her, confused by how she read my thoughts. "How did you even know?"

"Because Finn, you forget I have been here too. It's sadly a familiar situation in my line of work."

"How did it happen? I know people die. I have been deployed more than once. I've seen people die, but how does it happen for them? Do they just... I don't know. I don't know why I'm asking you this."

"I do," she said, shutting the door behind her. "If you would really like to know how it happened, I can tell you."

She sits down in the seat opposite to Dad, grabbing

his hand. "He called the bell. I was on a tea break and Jules came in here, but he wanted me. He was, he was, anxious. God, Finn, this is harder than I thought it would be." Her voice trembled as she tried to hold back her tears. After she took a moment to gather herself, staring down at his hands, she continued. "He was frightened –"

"You don't have to tell me it was disrespectful of me to ask." I interrupted.

"Oh Finn, don't be daft." She smiled in my direction, her eyes watery. "Jules came to find me and I put my dinner down thinking that he just wanted to tell me a random fact about boats or, you know, sometimes he just wanted to talk even if I couldn't understand him."

"Him and his boats." I smiled, giving her a glance while she gazed at Dad.

"Yes, him and those boats," she laughed. "Finn, when I came in here, he was acting very frightened. He wasn't… He wasn't fully coherent. He told me he was scared and I… I told him he didn't need to be scared. Oh god Finn, I'm sorry," she said, wiping the tears from her cheeks.

"I told him you loved him, Finn. I told him that of all the patients I have had, I thought you two were my most special. I told him you will be okay, and I will make sure of it. And then Finn, and then he looked at me and I told him it was okay to let go."

"And he just, let go?"

"He just went to sleep, Finn. He wasn't in pain, he was just scared. He didn't want to leave you, but he was ready; he was ready Finn."

I felt my eyes watering again as I gently placed my

hands over his free hand. Ainsley was right. He wasn't the ice cold I was expecting, which brought me a sense of comfort. For a moment, I envisioned he was simply sleeping.

"What happens now?" I questioned, catching Ainsley's eyes.

"Well, when you are ready, they will take him to the morgue downstairs and he will be transferred to the funeral home of preference."

I rubbed my hands down my face and blew out an exasperated breath. "I don't even know what he wants."

"As in his burial wishes?"

"Aye, he never told me."

"Did he not leave a will?"

"Aye, he did, but there is nothing in it. I asked him once, and he said just to throw him into the sea." The thought of that felt heartless and poetic in the same beat. It felt like I'd be tossing him aside and returning him home.

"Maybe Finn, maybe that is truthfully what he wanted?"

I shake my head. "No, I mean, well, isn't he meant to have a service?"

"Not always. You know, I didn't."

"You didn't?"

"Well, see my ma, she loved the Bray Cliff Walkway. She told me it was the only place she ever felt fully at peace by the ocean. So, Finn, I scattered her there. It was the only place I could ever envision as her last resting place."

"You really didn't have a service?" I questioned, wiping my cheek again.

Ainsley shook her head softly as she retreated her hand. "No, Finn I didn't. My mam, well she was an only child. We didn't have much family and those that we did well, they weren't close with us. I just..." she paused, taking a deep breath. "I just did it on my own, Finn, and I know, I know with certainty it would be what she would have wanted."

There was a moment's silence as we both stared at my father. It was hard not to feel as If I was in a dream, starting at life through frosted glass in a state of disconnect.

"I wanted to place him with Mum, but he never bought the plot, despite my mother insisting that he did. I thought maybe I could do it. You know where we scattered Lyall." I finally say, breaking the silence.

"Your brother, Lyall?" Ainsley questioned, shifting in her seat.

"Aye. We scattered him off the cliffs up by Bow Fiddle Rock. I don't know why it was there, but I feel the inside joke was that it was where he was conceived."

"Gee," Ainsley said, unsure of whether or not to laugh at the revelation. "Well, that's something."

"I don't know if you have ever been, but it is a pretty nice spot. Though, I doubt I will ever be able to look at it the same again and not just because of Lyall but the thoughts of my parent's..."

"I've never been, but now I am intrigued," Ainsley said with a grin as she placed a loose strand of hair behind her ear.

"I'll take you, you can tell me if you think it resembles

the top of a Bow Fiddle."

"The rock?"

"Aye, the rock."

She mulled over the question; her gaze fixed on my father. "And if it don't, will you hold it against me?"

"Of course not."

"Well, I think you have yourself a deal then."

There was a pause as we both stare at each other. In the silence, I could hear the faint sound of her breathing, her breaths quickened under my stare.

"I owe you a thankyou Ainsley, for everything."

"Finn, I'm just doing my job."

I shook my head. "It is more than that. You have been a good friend."

"A good friend? I never thought I would hear those words from you." She smiled before lifting the sheet over my father.

"Can I ask one thing?"

"Sure."

"I know you are sworn to professionalism and all now, but when I go to scatter him, I mean, could you come? I really don't know who else to ask, but I could always ask Blair –"

"No, it's okay, I don't mind." She interrupted me. "Happy to do that Finn, you just let me know when."

Guilt

For three nights, I barely slept. I was beyond exhausted, but I somehow lacked the ability to fall into a deep slumber. Each night I would lie there, recounting all that had happened over the last few months and before I knew I could hear the birds singing from outside.

"For fuck's sake," I groaned, burying my head into my pillow, feeling as if a freight train was running through my head.

I arranged with Ainsley to pick her up shortly after eight as we faced an hour and a half drive north to the rock and I knew she was starting her shift early afternoon.

I rolled myself out of bed and made my way to the bathroom, splashing my face, trying to soothe the grogginess. I stare into the mirror, studying my features, my eyes bloodshot with deep dark circles painting their edges, and my skin dry and flaky.

"God, you look dreadful," I muttered, splashing my face again.

I didn't know what to wear. A suit seemed ridiculous, yet jeans and a dress shirt felt too informal. I hit the wall in frustration, not strong enough to imprint the plaster, just hard enough to feel the sting of pain radiate up my knuckles.

"I don't know what I am fucking doing," I sighed, rubbing my temples furiously.

After debating for far too long, I ended up going with half a suit and half casual wear. I was in no state to be deciding such trivial things, and since I couldn't decide which way to go, I ended up just doing half and half.

When I arrived at Ainsley's flat, she was waiting for me outside, her back pressed against the wall, her head engrossed in a book. Dressed in jeans, white chuck tailors, and a pale-yellow chiffon blouse with her hair flowing down her shoulders. She looked gorgeous, even if I felt wrong for even thinking that.

Oblivious to my arrival, I watched her as the sun caught her hair, flushing it with vibrancy. Before I could honk, she looked up, catching my eyes and giving me a small wave before slipping her book in her bag.

"Get out," she said rather decisively as she opened the passenger door. "There is no way in hell I am letting you drive."

"Hello to you too," I said, surprised by her abruptness even if I knew she meant well by the grin that was spread across her face.

"Seriously, Finn, I value my life. I value it to a high degree actually, and by looking at you I can tell you haven't slept."

"Do I look that terrible?" I said jokingly as I unhooked my seat belt to switch sides.

"No, but you look like you are drunk or high and haven't slept in a week."

I let out a laugh, shaking my head. "You know how to get a man when he is down, don't ye."

Her tone changes and for a minute she looks at me, alarmed. "Finn I'm sorry I..."

"Calm down, would ye. I am just pulling your leg," I groan as I shuffle awkwardly over into the passenger seat.

"You realise you could have just got out?" she said, unimpressed as she made her way to the driver's side.

"That would require walking."

She lets out a laugh as she slides into the driver's seat. "I am glad to see you haven't lost your sense of humour just yet."

"Aye, never."

I learnt a lot about Ainsley as we made our way to the coast after picking up Dad's ashes, which had been placed into a small rectangle oak box. She told me of how she had never known her father and that most of her life her mum had spent working just to keep a roof over their heads. Her mother had her when she was fairly young and never could pursue her dream of becoming a Social Worker given she had limited family support. When Ainsley was in her last semester of studying nursing, her neighbour had called to say her mom was stark naked in the street in a state of confusion and a doctor diagnosed her the next day after Ainsley rang every specialist in Dublin.

Like Dad, her downhill slide was fast and within several weeks she was having to organise around-the-clock care for her mother while she desperately tried to hold it together to pass her final exams.

"It wasn't easy, Finn, I tell ye," she said as she glanced out at the rocky coastline when it came into view. "My relationship broke down shortly after because I couldn't give him my full attention, so he went and found that in someone else's arms. It was fine, though. I had sensed we would not be the happy ever after I had envisioned, but it still hurt." She let out a small gasp. "Oh gosh, I am so sorry. Why am I telling you all this?"

"It's fine," I said with a laugh, as it had come as a welcome distraction.

"No Finn, it's not. I don't know why I am telling you my life story when your dad…"

"Ainsley, it's fine."

She glanced at me, widening her eyes enough I could see the kaleidoscope of blues and greens in her irises. "It really isn't, but I will take your word for it." After a moment of silence, she let out an anguished laugh. "He was such an asshole."

"Who was?"

"My ex-partner. I am sure he has tainted my perception of men."

"How so?" I questioned, curious as to her rationale behind her confession.

"Well, for starters, I have dated no one since. It is far less complicated, that's for certain, but I think he scared me. I really loved him, Finn, and I realised you have no control of another's affections. You can give them your heart and soul and then they can shag up with Susan from the block."

"Her name Susan, was it?" I glanced at her, laughing as she squinted, focusing on the road.

"Oh god, no. Her name was Byrdie, and I thought she was my friend."

"Not everyone is your friend in life." I paused a second before deciding I was willing to share more of myself. "I haven't dated for a long time either."

"Why not?" She scrunched her nose after those words. "Sorry, that is none of my business. Here I am telling you mine."

I paused, captured off guard by her question. "I don't really know how to answer that. I think I just like to be alone. You realise for someone who I thought was one of the most optimistic people I have ever come across, you hold pessimistic views on love."

She laughed, pulling into the carpark. "Can I ask you something?" she whispered as she turned to me, unhooking her seatbelt.

"Sure." I stared at her, trying to gauge what question was coming next, but she gave nothing away in her neutral stare.

"How did he die? Lyall, I mean."

I stared down at the small box in my hands, running my fingers over its smoothed edges. "He died of that thing. You know where they die in their sleep for unknown reasons."

"SIDS?"

"Aye, that is the one. He was only a few months old. My da, he blamed himself, but I think it was just one of those things, you know?"

"That is truly awful, Finn, I'm sorry."

"You have nothing to be sorry for. It was just a sad accident. I guess it was the only place I could think of, as I knew he would drive out here sometimes. See, my mother, she..." I glanced at Ainsley briefly before turning my attention back to the sea, watching as it crashed into the rocky cliff face, sending sea spray in multiple directions. "She never wanted to talk about it. Dad, he hid his grief. I knew it affected him in ways he could never express to her, so he just hid it. Coming out here sometimes alone. I in the last twenty-four hours have asked myself why, but now I am here and I guess I kind of get it, you know. I can feel him here even though I never really knew him."

In words I could never articulate, I sensed a calming presence the minute the sea came into view. Something I thought would be an overwhelming experience was quite the opposite and, superstitious or not, it felt where Dad needed to be.

Ainsley studied my face, unmoving in her seat. "Do you know where you want to scatter him?" she finally asked gently, opening her car door.

I shook my head as I opened my door, embracing the crisp salted air before standing to assess our surroundings. "I think we will go up there," I said, pointing to the cliff face that looked down on the rock to the right. I could feel tears beginning well in my eyes. Even though I was calm, the reality of knowing that this was the end of the road weighed on me.

Ainsley, who had been staring out at the coast, turned

and faced me, and realising what was unfolding, quickly shut the car door and walked around to me, bringing me into her arms.

"I can't do this," I said shakily as I held onto Dad tightly.

"Finn, you can do this. We... We can do this."

"I don't think I'm ready. I..."

"If you would like to, we can go back. We can do this another time, Finn, it's not an issue."

"I... just I..."

"Finn, you don't need to do anything today. I mean it. We can go home. Take him home and you can process things a bit longer."

"No, I need to do this. I just... I don't know. I don't know why you are here. Why are you here?" I said, with the weight of what her presence meant. Friends help friends in times of distress, but the dynamic between us felt more intimate than friends.

"I'm here because I want to help you."

I shook my head in frustration, pushing back from her grasp. "I don't need any fucking help."

She said nothing, staring at me with a vacant expression, curling her lips tightly.

"You can leave, just leave." I demanded, gesturing towards the car, unable to look at her face.

"I'm not leaving you."

"Please, just fuck off would you."

"Is that really what you want?"

I stare at her, taking a deep breath tightening my hand into a fist. "I am so sorry. Ainsley, that was uncalled for."

"Don't be."

I was angry. I was frustrated. I was confused. Most of all, I was scared. Even though she was with me to help, she had to experience the full wrath of it.

"What do you want to do?" she questioned, putting her hand on her hip, looking at me; her expression softened.

"Let's just do this," I said with a sigh, making my way towards the trail that led to the cliff.

Once we got to the edge, we took a seat in the long grass, staring down at the ocean below.

Ainsley crossed her legs, placing her face into her palm as she gazed at me. "It really is a beautiful spot. All I can see is a rock, though."

I couldn't help but let out a laugh as I placed Dad to my right, giving her a playful smile. "Can you really not see it?"

"See what?"

"The resemblance?"

"I guess not," she said, dropping her hands and shrugging her shoulders. "I mean, I can kind of see it. Wait, no, I can't, I'm lying."

"You are a terrible liar, aren't you? Look," I said, pointing to the top of the rock. "It is the tip of a fiddle bow."

"Hm, I guess if you have a vivid imagination," she

said, smirking.

"I don't know what to do now." I glanced at her, avoiding eye contact. "What did you do?"

"When I scattered Mum's ashes, do you mean?"

"Aye."

"Well," she paused, biting her lip. "I talked to her. I told her I hoped wherever she was she wasn't suffering anymore and then I just did it. I was interrupted, as there were lots of people around that day. I think, maybe, if I had been there on my own, I would have sat there for hours. Do what you feel is right for you."

"He was a good man."

"I know he was, and you don't even have to tell me that. You can tell a lot about people in how they have raised their children, and he did a pretty good job with you."

"Are you trying to pick me up?" I joked, shooting her a grin.

"Oh, good grief Finn, not today." Her face flushed and even though the situation at hand was not the time to question it, I wondered what that meant. Not today.

"I know you mean well."

"Do you always have to turn everything into a joke?"

I tilt my head back, looking at the sky. "No, you are just easy to wind up." I took a moment to soak in the surroundings. The smell of the salty air, the crashing waves against the coastline, the gulls flying overhead. "I appreciate you being here."

"I'm glad you asked me."

There was a moment of silence, and everything between us seemed to shift. Exactly what I was afraid of when we pulled into the parking lot; the moment didn't feel like one between friends.

"I really don't know what else to say."

"Say what you feel and if you can't then say nothing."

"I guess. I'm grateful that I was lucky in life. So many people are born into situations where they never know what it is like to be loved as a child should. Even though he was away a lot, I always knew he loved me."

"What was your mum like?" Ainsley asked, picking a piece of long grass from her right twirling it in her fingers. "I know I asked before, but tell me something else about her and your dad."

"She was great. They loved each other so much." I paused, letting out a chuckle. "You know, they were just obsessed with each other. In some ways it used to make me so embarrassed, but they gave me an idea of what it is really like to love someone. Dad, before they both got sick, would always see each other on Tuesdays for as long as I could remember. When Dad wasn't at sea, they would always go for lunch on Tuesdays. It was their little thing. He loved her, in every meaning of the word, he loved her." I picked up Dad's boxed ashes. "I just can't believe he is gone. It's scary and I guess I don't know how to be on my own. Everyone else is married with kids now and I am the last one. Dad always wanted me to hurry. He was worried he was running out of time."

Ainsley looked at me, grinning. "I guess when you

have that expectation to live up to, how can you even compare to that?"

"Exactly," I laughed. "I mean, I'm sure what they had going on was of near miracle proportions."

"My mum, she never allowed herself to fall in love with anyone. I never knew why until she got sick when she confessed to me she would love no one the way she had loved my father. People assume that he just left, but it wasn't that. One day, he just disappeared. The town folk, in fact many people, said he had mental health issues, and they assumed he must have gone and taken his own life, but I think Mum believed he had a car accident or had come to some unfortunate end. He knew she was pregnant, and it was from my understanding he was excited to be a father. She knew he wouldn't have left us on purpose – not like that." She paused, grabbing her ponytail in her fingers, running her hands through it. "I know they were young and some would say dumb in the same sentence Finn, but my mum, she never moved on. I tried to find him for years, anything to give her some kind of closure. Found nothing and all it did was infuriate me."

"Look at us," I said, an influx of humour in my voice. "We are quite the pair."

"That we are."

There was a moment of silence again before I brought Dad into my hands. "I think I'm ready now."

Ainsley turned and looked at me, stunned. "Are you sure?"

"Aye, I am sure."

We made our way over to the edge, staring down at

the water below.

"This is a stupid question. Do I just tip it out?"

"Well, I guess that is what I did, but you could always, you know, do it by hand. Whatever you choose to do."

I slid the lid off, looking at the fine grey dust hidden inside. "Wow, this is..." My eyes welled with tears again, and Ainsley grabbed my hand, squeezing it gently.

"Take your time."

I inhaled a deep breath, closing my eyes before I tilted the box, then opening my eyes to see Dad becoming a wash with the sea breeze. All the emotions I thought I held back came to the surface again, and I felt a whole-body tremble.

Ainsley stroked my shoulders before embracing me again as I sobbed. "Don't hold it back Finn, just let it out."

Once I could bring my tears under control, I pulled myself away from her, looking directly into her eyes. Alone, in the mixed emotions of grief I found, my lips become locked with hers and not just as a one-off transgression. I lost the inability to pull myself from her as I slid my hand underneath her shirt, which caused her to gasp.

"Finn..." she said with a soft moan. "I'm sorry."

I could have taken her right then and there, but suddenly I felt myself fill with an enormous sense of guilt.

"Shit," I said out loud, pulling myself from her, leaving us both staring at each other, dazed and dumbfounded. "Ainsley. I'm... Oh god I'm sorry."

"Finn, it wasn't you, it was me I..."

"I... think we need to go," I said, sliding the lid back onto the box that had once contained my dad. The guilt was eating away at me, feeling as though I discounted the gravity of what I had done moments earlier. That day was meant to say goodbye to my father, and I allowed my emotions to take over.

We made our way back to the car, confused by what had just transpired. Neither of us said a word the whole journey back to Aberdeen. I wasn't sure what had just happened or whether Ainsley would ever talk to me again, but one thing was for certain: life was not done dealing its cards to me yet.

Game Changer

That night I lie awake, exhausted in every way imaginable. My head throbbed trying to digest all that had occurred that day and my eyes were stinging after not seeing any form of rest for nearly forty-eight hours.

My wayward thoughts drifted to Ainsley. Glancing at the clock, I knew she would finish her shift soon. Part of me wanted to message her an apology, but then part of me formed the assumption she would want me to leave her alone.

She kissed me back just as much as I kissed her. She never pulled away, and she certainly wasn't offended.

My thoughts were suddenly broken by my phone ringing, with Colin's name flashing on the screen.

"Ello mate."

"Finny, how was today?" Colin slurred into the receiver and I could tell he was drunk.

I paused, entertaining the thought of telling him before forming the realisation that was a terrible idea.

"It was fine – quick."

"Aye, that is good. Ye doing okay?"

"As good as I can be, I guess."

"Aye, that is good. I was just checking in with ye."

"Appreciate that, thank you. How's Blair?"

There was a pause, and I heard him take a large sip from the other end of the receiver. "He doing all right Finn. Once ye all sorted, I know he wants to see ya."

"For sure. Are ye okay? Ye have been drinking a lot lately." I glanced at the clock, feeling anxiety build about Colin, Blair, and the uncertainty with Ainsley.

"Stressed Finny, but it is nothing compared to what's happened with ye da. I'm going to be home next week so I'll come see ye."

I filed away Colin's comment about being stressed, not capable of diving into that conversation. "That'd be good."

"Ring if you need me?"

"Aye," I said in reply, ending the call before slumping back into my churned bed.

I only had another week of leave left before I was due back at work and I had to organise getting the house prepared for sale and get Dad's affairs in order. Work had been fairly understanding and offered me more time, but I was reluctant; I knew I needed to get back into my sense of normality.

Taking a deep breath, I closed my eyes, listened to the tick ricocheting from all four walls. I could feel my eyes becoming heavy, ready to fall into slumber before they were awoken by a single loud vibration from my cell phone placed on the bedside table.

"Fuck what now?" I said out loud, irrate in my state of

my fatigue.

Reaching over, staring at the glowing screen, I could see it was from Ainsley, and my heart raced.

Finn, I am so sorry about today. I hope you are okay?

Why was she sorry?

My nervousness turned to guilt because she had done nothing wrong, yet clearly felt she had. The day's events had become blurred in my incoherent state of weariness, but one thing was for certain: neither of us had put an abrupt stop to what had occurred.

"Well, this is fucking great," I murmured before letting out a sigh, staring down at the screen. I didn't know how to reply, but I wanted her to know in my eyes, she did nothing wrong.

You have nothing to apologise for. Thank you for coming today.

I placed my phone down on my chest, staring at the ceiling, remembering the way she laughed as I relayed to her about the intoxicating love of my parents. The way she laughed; the sound was so melodic that I knew I wanted to hear it again.

Another buzz of my phone on my chest alerted me to her response.

I am glad I could help. Are you sure you're okay? I could come and see you if you want me to. I worry about you being on your own today.

I knew seeing her was a bad idea given I envisioned her lying next to me, running my hands over her body, but found myself unable to prevent my response.

Actually, company would be good if you are free.

I knew I was playing with fire, as I was not after anything more than a friend, but I could not deny my attraction to her. I hadn't been in a relationship since Brianna – if you could call in that. I'd had a few onetime interactions with women since, but it was agreed upon that it would never be anything more.

In ways I couldn't articulate, I felt connected to Ainsley. Whether it was because our stories had similarities or because she showed me kindness and empathy when I was at one of my weakest points; I couldn't pinpoint it. She stirred feelings in me that felt so foreign but also brought a sense of calm. Even though I barely knew her, I wanted to know her. I needed to know her.

Be there soon.

Shit.

I panned my room, looking at the turbulent mess I had created that morning in my daze of trying to find something appropriate to wear. I shot up from bed to square away what I could, knowing I was on limited time.

A short while later, the front door buzzed, and I made my way down the stairs.

Upon opening the door, I saw Ainsley standing in jeans and a khaki jacket, shivering. "Gosh, it is freezing," she said, chattering with a smile.

"You best come in then, shouldn't ye?" I laughed as she nudged past me.

"You have a nice place. Not what I was expecting."

"Well, what were you expecting?" I asked as she slid

off her coat.

"Clearly not this." There was a period of awkward silence before she cleared her throat. "Look... About today I just, I just want to apologise. I don't know what happened. It should never have happened."

I felt a sense of tension creep on me. Her eyes were fixated on me as we stood in the hallway to the right of the stairs. I wanted to ask if she regretted it. I could feel the words on my tongue as I averted my gaze to the open windows in the lounge, watching a taxi collect a woman across the street.

"Finn, please say something."

"Do you regret it? Honestly?" the world tumbled out of my mouth unhinged, leaving her looking at me with furrowed eyebrows.

"Finn... I..."

"You don't have to answer that. I'm sorry I shouldn't be asking you that."

She took a step towards me. "The truth?" She glanced away, deep in thought, as if she seemed to question what she'd done, and her lip quivered. When she spoke again, her voice trembled. "No, I don't Finn, but it wasn't right. I should go. I don't know why I thought coming here was a good idea."

"I'm sorry. I didn't mean to upset you. I guess, I just needed to know."

"Know what?"

A surge of nervous adrenaline slowly entered my bloodstream as I did my best not to meet her stare, knowing I was one look away from having her up against the wall. "I needed to know I didn't force you. I wasn't thinking. It's all a fucking mess."

"It was both of us," she whispered, keeping her eyes downcast.

Don't do it.

"Ainsley, look at me."

Stop what you are doing, Finn. This is not a good idea.

"Ainsley, look at me, please."

As if she could feel the tension that was becoming clear, she kept her eyes low, fixating on her hands, and for a long time, the space was quiet. "I don't know what to say," she admitted before lifting her eyes to meet mine.

I edged myself closer to her, bringing her close, feeling the warmth of her body against mine.

"Finn, I...."

I could feel her run her hands through the thin fabric of my shirt before she wrapped them around my neck. The sensation of her touch was exhilarating; one that intoxicated me in its grip, and I leaned in to kiss her as she brought her mouth to mine.

There was a different passion to her kiss, something that made me feel vibrant and alive. I forced myself to pull back, to stop before we went too far, hoping I could prevent something I still wasn't sure was a favourable idea. I was full of hesitation, just as I had been earlier, but before I could dwell on it, she led me towards the couch, pulling me down with her.

This is not a good idea.

My breath quickened as I stared at her, and all at once, she leaned forward and lifted my shirt, exposing my chest.

"Ainsley I..."

She pauses for a moment, staring at me with her pale green eyes. "If you want to stop. We can stop."

I didn't want it to stop. I wanted her, but I also didn't want to ruin the friendship that had grown – one I appreciated in ways she would never know.

I gently nudged her off me, bringing myself to a stand. For a moment, I considered having the strength to end what I knew may become a regrettable decision. But I couldn't. I couldn't resist the primal urges that had taken over me. I pulled off my shirt, keeping my gaze firmly on her before unbuckling my jeans and letting them hit the floor.

With my focus on Dad for quite some time, it had been a while since I indulged in anything for myself. Too long since I thought about what I wanted and nothing else. I wanted her.

Whether or not I would come to regret that decision wasn't my concern. For that moment, it was everything I needed and that, well, that was all that mattered.

Sometime later I awoke with Ainsley asleep next to me. I stared at her, watching as her body rose with every inhalation. Everything about her was sensationally peaceful, but I couldn't escape the lingering sense of dread within me. As much as I had desired her, I couldn't help wondering whether there had been a trace of desperation in our indulgence.

I rolled over, staring at the ceiling with my thoughts drifting to Brianna and why I felt I could never commit myself to her. I felt if we labelled it, the relationship would change. As time passed and I matured, I realised I just wasn't that into her and she didn't make me feel the way Dad had always described.

Before Dad got sick, he and I drove up north to purchase a model train set he insisted on buying, much to my mother's displeasure. She had just received her diagnosis and the financial penalty of her not working, I knew, was on her mind.

As we journeyed our way north, Dad, as he had often asked me before, questioned when I was going to settle down.

"I haven't found 'the one' yet," I said with a laugh.

"You'll know when you do," he replied as he lost himself in thought.

"Aye, will I? How will I know da, because I'm not doing too well in that department."

He briefly glanced at me before turning his attention back to the road. "Everything with your person you meet in this life, whoever that is, will seem so effortless. I remember..." he paused, letting out a brief chuckle. "I remember when I first met your ma, and she was quite the looker in her day, I tell ye. But talking to her, Finn, I felt like I had known her for a hundred years. Of course, it was the fact that she could sink a pint all whilst dancing on a table faster than any of us that did it for me in the end. Aye, I'll never forget that."

Nobody I had ever met felt effortless. Brianna and I,

we had fun, but we were not compatible. She had the personality and sense of humour of a fence post – something that caused a great deal of arguments.

I glanced over at Ainsley, who was stirring in her sleep, and I reflected on Dad's words. I had only known her just shy of a month, but I felt I had known her my whole life. The way she laughed, the way she touched me, it did things to me no one else had over done. But as she slept next to me, I couldn't for the life of me figure out why. What was the difference between her and every other woman?

Come morning, I was going to have to tell her that if she was seeking something more than a casual shag that I couldn't be that for her. It filled me with a sense of guilt, as I didn't want to hurt her, and without her expressing this to me, I knew it was going to.

I took in a deep breath before letting out a sigh. *What have I done?*

My sigh stirred her, and she rolled over to face me. "Finn, are you okay?" she said, nearly inaudible.

I placed my hand on her shoulder, feeling the smooth warmth of her skin under my hand. The very touch of her caused my heart to quicken and my breath to quiver.

"Aye, I'm okay," I whispered. "It's still early. Go back to sleep."

With a sheepish glance she smiled, "Finn, I need to tell you something."

"Go on."

Please don't make this harder on me, Ainsley.

"I feel like an idiot saying this but, Finn, I think you are great," she mumbled, running her hand over my torso, which set my skin alight with goosebumps.

Fuck, please don't tell me this.

I felt a knot in my stomach. I could have easily told her I thought she was great too, but I knew that would only complicate matters come morning. Instead, I said nothing, gently planting a kiss on her left cheek. "Go back to sleep."

"I am. Good night," she whispered with a soft smile as she retreated her hand.

For a moment, I watched her as I bathed in my guilt. I could lie with her for the rest of my being and not tire from the way she tasted or felt. But I knew I could never fully give myself to her in the way she not only needed, but the way she deserved.

I knew I was going to have to explain that to her whilst trying to inflict the least damage possible, but as I watched her sleep, I so desperately wished it wasn't so.

The Visit

The following morning I awoke to Ainsley gliding her hands over my shoulders.

"Good morning, you," she whispered, placing a cup of coffee on the bedside table.

"Morning," I replied, my voice shaky. "What time is it?"

"Just after eleven."

"Wow, how long have you been awake for?"

"Since eight. I didn't mind though I just showered and had some breakfast. You really need more food in your cupboards."

"I know, I'm sorry. Did you find anything edible?" I did my best to avert my eyes from hers by staring at my coffee, but she could sense something was wrong.

"Finn, are we okay?"

I took a loud sip of coffee, holding it against my lips.

"Finn…"

I glanced at her, realising she had slipped on one of my shirts, wearing nothing underneath, and I felt my heart race.

"Nice shirt," I joked, doing my best to avoid the question.

"This old thing? Really? You like it," she teased, taking a seat next to me.

I ran my tongue over the top of my mouth, trying to divert my attention from her exposed legs. "Ainsley..."

"Finn?"

"About last night..."

"Finn, I know you want nothing. You're not seeking anything. I'm not seeking anything. We are adults."

"I was just going to say I'm going back to work next week so..."

"Finn, it's fine, I understand."

Part of me could sense there was disappointment in her words. The way she spoke was in contrast to her normal, joyous tone.

"Ainsley..."

She lowered her gaze, turning away from me.

"Ainsley, I don't want to hurt you."

"Finn, I'm not looking away because I'm deeply in love with you and I'm heartbroken that you never want to see me again."

"I never said I never wanted to see you again."

She let out a nervous laugh. "Well, that's something."

"Why won't you look at me?"

"Because Finn." She paused, biting her lip. "Because, Finn, I can't look at you right now without wanting to..." She brought her hand to her face, obscuring her view. "Is it wrong that I find you attractive?"

I placed my coffee down on the table, unable to stop myself from pulling her towards me.

I knew it was a mistake, but I couldn't help myself. It had been so long since I had been with someone; I wanted to savour the sensation she gave me, regardless of the consequences. Before I could form a rational thought, we were once again in a tangle of sheets.

∞∞∞

I decided I was going to go visit Blair and relay what happened with Ainsley as we searched for her wayward shirt.

"The best thing you can do is to be there for him," she said, lifting one of the couch cushions.

"I have no idea where this shirt is," I said, laughing as I lie flat on the ground to see if it had somehow slipped underneath the sofa.

"I'm sure it will show up, eventually."

"Are you hungry? I could really use some food."

"Well, I could make you something if you like? I mean, I really don't want to leave here without knowing you have something other than mouldy bread and crackers in your cupboards."

"You realise I am going back to work in a few days?"

"Yes, you said."

"So why would I need food?"

"For when you come back?"

Her words hit me harder than I expected they would. With Dad gone, I had no reason to come back to Aberdeen unless I was simply wanting to escape Edinburgh.

"Did I say something wrong?" she questioned, confused by my silence.

"No, no, not at all. I guess just weighing up whether I will keep this old place." I waved my hands around, trying to distract from my internal debate.

"Oh." She turned away and appeared bothered by our conversation's turn.

"I bought this flat, basically just to have somewhere to stay. Mum and Dad's house was far too big for me, so we put tenants in it. I guess I never thought about what happens now. I kinda like this place, you know? But, I don't want it sitting empty for months on end."

"Well, I hope you come back. At least, sometimes because who else am I going to hang out with?"

"Shock horror. You might have to make some friends," I said, laughing.

She narrowed her eyes at me. "I don't need friends."

"Everybody needs friends."

"I don't."

"Yes, yes you do, given your apparent lack of social skills and, must I add, sleeping with the patient's family. People can get struck off the register for such things."

She stared at me, placing her hand on her hip.

"You're different."

"How am I different?" I held her stare, raising my eyebrow.

"You are my friend."

"And you sleep with all your friends, do you?"

She threw a cushion in my direction. "You are really not funny, you know that?"

"I might come back and visit you, if you're lucky."

"Well, Finn, they say, luck of the Irish, you know?"

I tried not to laugh. "Tell me you did not just say that?" She glared at me with a smile, desperate to escape her fixed lips before we both burst out in laughter. "Are you working today?"

"Not today."

"Do you... Do you want to come with me to see Blair? I guess it would just be nice to have some company."

"And you think I am adequate company?"

"Well, you are better than no company."

She spun away, continuing to look for her wayward shirt. "I don't know how I feel about that response. I feel I am inclined to decline on that basis."

"What do you want me to say then?"

"Tell me you want my company."

"Ainsley," I said, smirking. "I want your company should you feel inclined to give me the pleasure."

The guilt I felt last night seemed to become diluted in Ainsley's words that we were adults. The previous night should have meant nothing. In the morning, it was just two friends who found each other attractive. However, I couldn't escape from the feeling her laughter gave me. The sensations I had when she smiled and the joy I felt in the absurdity of her jokes. I had never fallen for anyone to know what that felt like, but as the day progressed, it became evident I just wanted to be around her.

As we made our way south to Blair, Ainsley confided to me she had never been to Edinburgh. Whilst I knew she wasn't seeking an invitation, I found myself asking her if she would like to come and stay.

Last year I bought a run down two-bedroom flat in the city centre. It was on the top floor with a small patio that, on a clear night, you could see half of the city below.

"I would, Finn, I would love that. I've heard so much about Edinburgh."

"Well, come down for a weekend then," I said, making the right-hand turn down Blair's street.

Blair's mother answered the door, looking intrigued by Ainsley's presence. "Finn, I have not seen you in so long," she chirped, squeezing me tightly, tainting my clothing with the smell of Winfield Reds.

"Ainsley, this is Blair's mum Gillian."

"Nice to meet you."

"Come in, come in, you two. Blair is in the lounge."

As we entered their hallway lined with pictures of Blair and his four sisters, I heard Blair's familiar voice call out from their lounge to the right. "Aye Finny!" he called, standing to greet us.

"And... hello?" he said, turning to Ainsley, looking surprised before giving me a wide-eyed expression.

"You remember Ainsley don't you?"

"Aye I do." He smirked.

"So how are ye?" I questioned as we took a seat.

"Finny, I don't know what to tell ye, man. I wasn't thinking. I just got overwhelmed. It's all in here and I'm trying to run from it," he said as he grasped his head with both hands. "Just got me ye know."

"You need to seek help. It will help. I know you think it won't but it will."

"Aye, but I've lost Shell. I pushed her away, Finny. She got fed up with it all. How am I meant to get her back?"

I shrugged, not knowing how to offer reassurance, but opted for honesty. "Maybe you aren't meant to. Regardless, you can get through this."

"Finny, you ain't ever been in love before. Of course you would say that. I will get her back somehow."

I could feel Ainsley's eyes on me after Blair's words poured out and for some unknown reason, it made me flustered. "Your right I haven't but I also know that in time you'll see that if she don't come back, life goes on."

"I'm not even going to answer that." Blair replied, shaking his head as he gave Ainsley a brief glance. "I'll be right, Finny. Now, how are ye? I'm sorry about ya da man."

"We knew it was coming. Just grateful it was peaceful, you know?"

"Aye, that is good."

"Where is the loo?" Ainsley asked, tapping me gently on my knee.

"It is the second door on the right," Blair interrupted, pointing down the hallway.

After Ainsley excused herself, Blair seized the opportunity to interrogate me in the little time he had. "Aye, ye sly one yew." He took a seat on the sofa as I sat in an armchair on the opposite side of the room.

"You have it wrong, ye dafty. We are just friends. Don't start this again."

"Aye, no. Friends do not look at each other like the way she looks at yew."

"Nay. All in your head, man."

"Aye Finny, if you don't see it ye blind."

The guilt that had evaded my conscious thoughts surged its way through me as I stared at Blair. "I can't be with her," I snapped.

"Why the fuck not? She's hot man."

"Aye, she is, but it's not that."

Blair leaned forward in his chair, resting his elbows on his knees. "Don't you enjoy her company?"

"Fuck's sake man, of course I do or she wouldn't be here."

"Then tell me Finny, tell me why, because she is as good as you will ever get."

I stared at Blair, faced with the question I had asked myself over and over since last night. "I can never fall in love with her."

Blair shook his head, taking a sip of his tea. "Well Finny me lad, I think that is your choice and not simply a matter of can't." Perhaps Blair was right, but our conversation was interrupted by the sound of the front door slamming and Ainsley hastily making her way down the path. "Ar fuck, she must have heard you Finny."

I paused for a moment, unsure of what the expectation of me was.

"Are ye not going to go after her?"

I darted through the front door after her. By the time I reached Ainsley, she was halfway down the road with tears streaming down her face.

"Ainsley, please stop," I yelled as I ran after her.

"Finn, please just leave me alone."

"Ainsley please, let me explain."

"I don't want your explanation Finn. Just leave me alone!"

"Ainsley stop."

She glanced over her shoulder before walking faster.

"Ainsley" I grab her hand and she halted. "Please listen to me."

"This was a mistake; I just want to go home."

I fumbled over my words, not knowing how to explain to her what my reasoning was. "It's not you. Okay, Ainsley I... If I could, you would by far be the least objectionable person to fall in love with but I..."

Tears were streaming down her face, and I hated I upset her. "You owe me nothing Finn so don't even bother explaining."

"Ainsley, I promise it's not you."

"Okay, well enlighten me since you insist on explaining to me." She let out a laugh, shaking her head in frustration, not giving me a chance to speak. "You know, Finn, I lied to you this morning. I could see on your face that you weren't feeling it, so I did my best to hold it together, but Finn, I..."

"Ainsley."

"I think about you all the time. I realised there was something the night we went to dinner. I started waiting for you to arrive at work. Wearing makeup, feeling nervous when you were around. And I knew, Finn, I knew last night that... Well Finn, I love you. And I know that because nobody has made me feel the way you did last night. Nobody makes me laugh the way you do. I feel so effortlessly happy in your presence. I'm an idiot and I should never have come to your house last night, but I know, I know you feel it too. I know you have your ideas, but you don't see the most important thing in life, do you? To be truly known and loved by someone you've chosen. You could choose me. You could make a choice."

"Ainsley, I..." I couldn't find the words, and in a state of panic, I made my way back to the car. I knew escaping the situation was the only way I could try to cause the least amount of hurt to her.

"Finn, where are you going?"

I kept my head low, unable to turn around and face her.

"Finn, please don't walk away from me."

Blair was standing in the doorway, watching as I made my way straight for the car.

"Please make sure she gets home safe," I said in a

rushed slurred tone, keeping my head fixed in its downward stare. So much had happened in the last three days; I needed to escape.

For some reason, I made my way to the exact spot where Mum had told me she was dying. It had been years since I'd been on that stretch of road, but the sense of familiarity came back in waves as I passed through each small town laced with memories of what I felt a lifetime ago.

As I brought the car to a stop, I could do nothing but cry.

She was gone. Dad was gone. I was alone, but I had the choice to not be if I wanted to, but for the life of me, I struggled to understand why I couldn't accept it.

A White Lie

The day my mother told me she was sick, I had sensed something wasn't quite right. Given I had mainly been raised by my mother in my father's absence, I clicked onto her inability to lie when I was quite young. She had always been someone who would look directly at you during conversation and, as intimidating as it may be for some, you always knew when you had her full attention.

The day prior she avoided something she had never done and when pressed for what was wrong she couldn't look at me as she gave me short indirect replies.

"Do you want to tell me what is going on?" I questioned for the third time as I made myself a cup of tea.

She was furiously mopping the floor, filling the air with the stench of bleach. "Nothing" she replied, keeping her head fixed low as glided the mop back and forth appearing agitated,

"Ma, I know you," I replied, giving her a glare.

"And I know you Finn, so drop it." She returned a brief glance at me as she wrung out the mop.

I nodded in reply, respecting that whatever it was, she didn't want to discuss it. The following morning, that changed when she seized an opportunity by insisting I go with her into the city.

After we finished our errands, we pulled into Tullos Hill and she insisted we go for a walk.

"Come on," she said as she opened the car door. "We need to talk."

Growing up in Aberdeen, you learn about the rich history the hill has buried in its woodland and wildflowers. In the Bronze Ages it was a burial site before becoming an Anti-Aircraft Battery in WWII. Once we got to the top, staring out at the wind farm offshore, the words fell out of her mouth. The last time my mother and I had been there was when she had to tell me our dog wouldn't be coming home from the vet when I was twelve years old, so I sensed whatever was coming wasn't good.

My mind was racing, questioning if perhaps she and my father were getting divorced, or they were having financial troubles since my father retired. Not once did I ever consider what she was about to say.

"Finn, I have something to tell you." She paused as she took a deep breath, unable to look at me.

"What is it?" I questioned, panic in my voice. Given the anguish in her own, I knew whatever it was had to be serious.

"I'm dying," she mumbled.

I froze before letting out an uncontrollable, nervous laugh. "Don't joke like that Ma."

There was a moment of silence where she smoothed the stones with her foot before she took a deep breath to brace herself. "I'm not joking Finn. I have terminal bowel cancer."

I stared at her. Tears had run down her cheeks. "No..."

What is she talking about? I watched as she brought her hand to wipe her tears.

"There is nothing they can do, and I need to tell you before I tell your father. He is going to need you. I know you haven't always seen eye to eye, but he is going to need you."

"Ma..." I stammered. "How long?"

"Months. They think, at best, six to nine."

"There must be something they can do."

She shook her head, walking several steps away from me with her gaze fixed on the ground. "There is nothing they can do. It is everywhere."

I walked towards her and wrapped my arms around her tightly as we both cried. It would take me months to accept her diagnosis, but I knew at that very moment just by telling me the diagnosis had finally sunk in for her.

Once we had stemmed our emotions, we sat down, staring out to the coast, and she told me all she wanted to do before she passed. In the thick of it, we were both highly emotive, with my mother often pausing to compose herself.

"I'm not ready, my sweet boy," she whispered as she grabbed my face in her hands.

"I'm not ready. I have so much I want to do. I wanted to see you get married, hopefully one day. Grandkids everything."

I sniffled, my lip trembling. "You didn't deserve this Ma."

"Nobody deserves it, unfortunately things happen that we have no control over. That is the beauty and the ugliness in life."

"When will you tell dad?"

"When I am ready."

I nodded, giving her hand a squeeze. "Will you be okay?"

"No, but I have to be. We will make it count. If I know I am going out soon, I best do that with a bang."

"I would expect nothing less, Ma." I replied, giving her a forced smile.

It was a moment in time I will never forget. It was my last memory of her before the illness really took hold. As I found myself back at that same spot, the scenery looked no different, but so much had changed.

I took a deep breath, staring out at the coast where the wind turbines were rhythmically fluttering in the breeze. I knew I could love Ainsley easily because part of me already did; but I couldn't commit to her. Knowing how I felt after I knew I was losing my mother and seeing the destruction that caused my father, I couldn't.

I felt as if I had not only let myself down but my mother, father, and Archie down too. I closed my eyes, taking a deep inhalation of the salted air, questioning what my mother would say.

She would have loved Ainsley, I knew that as fact. They were too much alike for me to even doubt that she wouldn't. I wouldn't survive losing her, too, and I knew I had no control over that. Knowing how it felt when I lost my mother, my father and everyone else I had lost, why would I put myself through that? I couldn't. I wouldn't.

Maybe we'd drift apart, back to the strangers we were many months prior. Maybe she would forgive me in time, and we could be friends. It wasn't as if I wanted to hurt her, but in the aftermath of my actions, I already had.

Saying goodbye would be one of the hardest thing I ever had to do. Part of me wanted to turn the car around and race back to her, to tell her I would always be there for her, to confide in her the things I knew I felt. But I couldn't.

I made my way back to the house to pack and make my way back south. I was numb and as I made my way out of town; it was as if I was on autopilot. Part of me never wanted to talk to her again, but at the same time, I longed to confide in her. I wanted to turn the car around more than once, or at least call her, only I didn't.

When I arrived in Edinburgh, it felt clouded in forgiveness. With all that had happened in Aberdeen, I had nearly forgotten that I had a separate life. One that had to continue as if what happened back home never had.

Once I unpacked, I submerged myself into the sofa and stared at my phone. I needed to call Blair, but my stomach felt pitted at the very thought. Throughout our friendship, there had been many times when we disappointed each other, but we never held grudges. Somehow, I felt he would struggle to accept my choice, and maybe even resent me and the impact my decision would have. He always respected women greatly and what I had done to Ainsley wasn't respectful. No, it was downright cowardly and heartless.

I let out a sigh as I dialled his number to prepare for the onslaught I could see coming, but to my surprise, Blair was relatively calm.

"Finny," he muttered through the phone, and I heard a door shut behind him in the background.

"Is she okay?" I questioned, picking nervously at the tan-coloured leather cushions.

There was a moment of silence when I waited for him to speak. "How do you think she is? She is a mess. I mean, Finn, really? We waited two hours for you to come back before I had to tell her you weren't. She still believed you would come back, even after I told her. Where did you go? Where are you now?"

"I'm back in Edinburgh," I replied quietly.

"Wait, what? No."

"Aye, I arrived here about an hour ago."

"So that is just it then, is it?" The calm in his voice was fast disappearing and with it, the guilt of my actions surged through me. "Well...?"

I said nothing in reply, unsure of what I was meant to say.

"Are you really going to leave it like this? I knew you were always a bit of an arse, but not like this."

"It's not what I had done intentionally. It was never my desire to hurt her."

"Then what did you want, Finny? Because it beats me."

"I..." I stammered.

"I'm not going to press it. It is your choice even if I think you are making a mistake. She is fine. Maybe not right now, but she will be. Are you okay?"

"I'm fine."

"Of course you are," Blair replied with a sarcastic laugh.

"What does that mean?"

Blair paused, and I could hear him light a cigarette in the background. He had spent the better part of two years fully coming off them. I felt a pang of guilt in the consideration perhaps I had driven him to start again. "You are always fine. It is just who you are. I mean fuck, when you were dealing with all the shit in your head, nobody knew. It's not healthy, but it's none of my business, is it?"

"We don't all show emotions like you do," I retorted, feeling the urge to defend myself under his scrutiny.

"But you show no emotions, Finn. That's part of your

problem. Anyway, I have to go help Ma with something. Call her, eh?"

I told a white lie saying I would but the minute he hung up I knew I wouldn't. She tried to reach out to me first by text messages I moved to an archive folder on my phone. Then she sent a letter which I crumbled and threw in the bin without opening it. Two hours later, I went to retrieve the letter, but it was too late and the bins had been cleared. I will never know what was hidden in the words of that envelope, but it would have been unlikely to change the course of our relationship.

Blair only brought it up on two occasions, suggesting I go home. But I didn't go, and I didn't call. I didn't write her back, nor did I hear from her again.

Edinburgh

A year passed, and I had actively avoided communicating with anyone. Life fell into a routine where I went to work, ate, and slept. I thought about Ainsley more often than not, unable to shake the guilt that was rattling every fibre of me. I missed her. The way she made me feel, the way she made me laugh. I thought it would eventually wither and suppress, but it never did. The absence, the void in my life she filled only grew over time till it reached a point I could no longer ignore it.

One afternoon, I looked at my phone, deleting old messages from my inbox. My heart sank as I accidentally opened the archive folder with the unopened messages Ainsley had sent the week after I fled Aberdeen.

Finn

I realise you don't want to talk to me and that is fine.

I am sorry. I never wanted this. I have only ever wanted you to be happy. I miss you, I miss everything about you.

If you can find it within yourself to forgive me, please call.

I can't stop worrying whether you are okay.

Ainsley.

I stared down at my screen, fighting the urge to call her. So much time had passed, but it felt as if it had all happened yesterday. Our lives had continued in separate directions, two spokes on a wheel, but part of me knew our lives would always be intertwined. After a period of hostile internal debate, I eventually succumbed, nervously dialling her number.

After three short rings, she answered. The very sound of her voice sent a shiver down my spine. "Hello?"

I paused, feeling a lump in my throat, unsure of what to say next. "Ainsley, hi." I croaked, my voice barely recognisable.

I listened as she breathed out heavily into the receiver. "Why are you calling me?" she questioned.

"Look, I –"

"It has been months. I have moved on. I'm sure you have too. I don't really want to do this, Finn." I could sense a hint of agitation in her voice, and I couldn't blame her for that.

"Ainsley, I was wrong, I made a mistake."

"I did too. Clearly."

I didn't know what love was – at least, not what it felt like – but I accepted I loved her given my inability to let her go, even after all the time that passed.

"Ainsley, I..." I stammered, unable to form a sentence.

"Finn, I do not want to do this. So if you don't mind,

I think I'll just go."

"Ainsley, please, just wait…"

"Finn, what? What do you want?"

I froze, unsure if my feelings would be reciprocated anymore. "I think, Ainsley… I think I love you."

There was a moment of silence which felt like years as I waited for her to say the words, only she didn't. "Finn, I'm sorry I…"

"Well, this is not how I thought it would be," I muttered.

She took a deep breath. I could hear the softest tremble in her words, a suspicion that she was feeling the exact emotion I was at that moment. "Finn, look, can I see you?" she finally said, her voice becoming distant.

"I am in Edinburgh. Do you want me to come to you?"

She paused, thinking for a moment. "No, I think it is best that I come to you. Can you text me your address? I'll head down this afternoon?"

"Will do."

I closed my eyes once I was alone with my thoughts, thinking back to when I had encouraged her to come to Edinburgh. I remembered the way her eyes lit up, the corners of her mouth slightly creased. A moment that was filled with such promise became one now that filled me with the bitterness of my actions.

I spent the afternoon cleaning my flat that had, just like me, become a passenger of time, merely surviving with the cobwebs and dust that had become comfortable in the corners.

Ainsley arrived just after seven that evening, dressed in a forest green coat and leather boots. She barely spoke, her mind adrift elsewhere as she took a seat. "I brought wine," she said, reaching into her bag. "Would you like a glass of wine?"

I shook my head. "I've never been much of a wine drinker."

She stood, walking over to the kitchen, opening the cupboards to find a glass.

"You've changed," I observed.

She shrugged. "A lot of things have changed since I last saw you."

She said nothing more and walked back to the couch. When she spoke again, her voice was subdued. "I never thought I'd be the person who looked forward to a glass of wine in the evenings, but now I do." She stared down at the glass, swirling its contents, and I wondered what had happened to her. "You know the funny thing?" she said. "It doesn't make me happy like others claim it does. Well, Finn, it makes me feel calm. I seem so on edge all the time now, I well, I can't understand why."

I didn't fully recognise the woman who sat before me, and I wasn't sure how to respond.

"Don't get me wrong," she went on. "I don't need it. My mother was an alcoholic. It just helps sometimes."

I smiled at her philosophy, understanding how unfair it was to cling to the time-capsule version I held of her. "I am not judging you."

"I know," she said. "But I think for a moment you were wondering." For a moment, the only sound in the kitchen was the low purr of the refrigerator. "I'm sorry about your dad," she said, tracing a crack in the table-top. "I really am. I can't tell you how many times I've thought about him and you over the last year."

"Thank you," I said.

Ainsley began rotating her glass again, lost in the swirl of liquid. "Do you want to talk about it?"

"Do I want to talk about my father? No, I want to know why you're here."

She placed her glass down, looking at me inten-sively. "Finn, this was difficult for me. I mourned for you for months. I tried to call you. I reached out to Blair but eventually I had to form the assumption you wanted nothing more to do with me."

"I was an idiot."

"We both were Finn, but I've met someone. Some-one who makes me happy. Finn, he makes me happy and I..." She paused, and I turned away, trying to di-gest her words. We sat in silence for a while, each of us wrestling with our thoughts. "Anyway, I felt I needed to tell you in person," she concluded. "I don't know how much more you want to hear."

I wasn't sure, either. "Does he know you are here? Why are you here? Did you come all this way just to tell me that?" I questioned, becoming irritated.

"Of course he doesn't."

"Do you think that's wise?"

She scowled at me, placing her glass down. "You want to lecture me about morals?"

"Don't…" I shook my head. "Let's not go there."

"Why?" she asked. "Do you regret it?"

"What do you think I am going to say?" I couldn't bear to look at her. "Of course I do. But you have moved on, isn't that why you're here?"

"I just needed to see you," she said. "I can't forget it. Do you want me to?"

"I don't know," I said. "Maybe."

"I can't," she said, sounding surprised and hurt by my answer.

"If he makes you happy, that is all I could wish for you, Ainsley."

She pressed her lips together. "I'm sorry," she murmured.

"I am, too." I tried to smile – I failed. "If you want my honest opinion, I think you should have waited for me."

She laughed, and I was surprised by the look of longing on her face as she reached for her glass of wine. "I've been thinking about that, too. Where we would have been, where we'd be living, what we'd be doing in our lives. Especially lately, since I met Evan, I've been trying to convince myself that even if you had felt the same, it never would have lasted."

I paused, realising it was the first time she had said his name. "I think we would have."

The past loomed over us, overwhelming in its intensity.

"I don't love him like I know I would've loved you. He is a good man, Finn. I can't hurt him. I feel so conflicted. After you called, you are all I could think about. I have tried to shake you but I can't."

I had never been one to pursue a taken woman but I couldn't fight the urge of wanting to take Ainsley in my arms, to hold her, to recapture everything we had lost in our year apart. Instinctively, I leaned towards her.

She didn't fight it either and before we realised, we made our way to the bedroom.

∞∞∞

The following morning when I awoke, Ainsley was absent. Her clothes still lay strewn across the room.

I made my way down the stairs, dressed in nothing but a pair of white cotton boxer shorts, to find her seated on the couch cradling her knees. I knew what was coming based on her expression.

"We can't do this again," she said, avoiding my gaze.

"Well, what was last night? Ainsley, what was last night for? Did you just want to have the last laugh or what?" I should have comforted her, but I couldn't fight the frustration I was feeling.

"Of course I didn't. Don't be so immature."

"Well, what was it then?"

"I can't hurt him Finn; I won't do it. He doesn't deserve it and clearly I don't deserve him." She lowered her head to her knees, refusing to look at me.

"And you think he wouldn't be hurt if he knew what you did?"

"He is never going to know, is he? I mean, he doesn't even know where I am right now." I was surprised by the anger in her voice as she stood, pacing back at forth.

"So you want to start a life with him based on secrets and lies? Is that it?"

"It was a mistake coming here."

"We seem to make a lot of those, don't we?" I snapped.

We stood there facing each other with only the three seater couch separating us. Her lips were parted, and she lifted her chin. I wanted to cross the room and go to her, knowing that she wanted me as much as I wanted her. But I stayed where I was, frozen by the thought that she would one day hate me for what we both so clearly desired.

"I don't expect you to understand Finn."

"Good, because I don't." I patted my pocket, pulled out my keys, and turned to leave, feeling tears burning at the back of my eyes.

"Where are you going?" Ainsley questioned, watching me walk away.

"I am going out for the morning. I trust you will be gone by the time I return."

Ainsley said nothing, and I briefly glimpsed her face with tears streaming down her cheeks. That wasn't how I ever envisioned our first time in Edinburgh together would go, but life has a funny way of not giving you what you want.

I took a deep breath as I stumbled down the stairs, wondering just how life could have been different if only I had picked up the phone.

365 Days

Ayear after I had last seen Ainsley, I found myself back seated in the small fluorescently lit psychologist's office once more. She hadn't called and I don't know why I expected she would. With each day that passed, I remained convinced that maybe she would wake up and realise it was me she wanted. But she never did and as a result, I sank further into depression. Work had become concerned about my lethargic and unmotivated demeanour, questioning if I was depressed and Blair was convinced I was close to becoming the next casualty in a long list of comrades who could no longer see the value in their life.

While I was reluctant, I accepted I needed help and agreed to six sessions with Dr Kent.

Dr Kent was someone I had grown to know quite well, given he helped me navigate my PTSD upon returning from Afghanistan. Even though it had been nearly three years since I had seen him last, he still looked the same with his clean-shaven face and greying hair slicked to the right of his aesthetically perfect square jaw.

"Finn, how are you? It has been a while," he said with a smile on his face. "Do take a seat."

For the last year, all three hundred and sixty-five days, I felt I had lost a piece of me I never knew existed. While I was doubtful that seeing Dr Kent again would do me any benefit, I longed to feel the me who existed before Ainsley came into my life. If you had asked me three years ago if I ever believed that I would have been back in this office, only this time discussing a woman I seemed unable to let go of, I would have told you that you were mad. Yet, there I was, desperate to move on and find myself again.

"What brings you here?" he questioned, leaning back in his red leather chair.

I hesitated. How was I even meant to describe the situation to him when I didn't know it myself? "I don't feel like myself." I replied vaguely, fidgeting with my hands.

"What do you mean you don't feel like yourself?"

I pause, fixed on a framed black and white poster of Albert Einstein on his wall. "I feel like I'm not getting any enjoyment out of life anymore, but it's not what happened over there, doc; I'm good there."

"Okay," he said with a nod. "What is going on?"

As I relayed the story of Ainsley, how we met and what happened, he did nothing but stare at me with an expression I could not decipher.

"How is your hygiene?"

Watching Archie spiral into depression, I had a front-row seat to how hygiene played a role in the signs of depression. I also learned that hygiene was not simply a matter of brushing teeth and showering. What Dr Kent was really asking for was if I was sleeping, eating, and laying off the drink.

"I'm doing okay. That is not the problem. I just want to

forget her."

"Why would you want to forget someone who clearly made you happy, Finn?"

I stared at him, unsure of his response. Even though I knew deep down he was right, pondering his question only made me confused.

"See, that there lies the problem. Letting go of the grief..."

I raised my hand to interrupt him, annoyed by his assumption. "I'm not grieving, that is not it."

"Finn, I think it is. I know that may be hard for you to hear, but if you want to move on from this, part of that process will be recognising the feelings attached to the situation. How are you feeling? Angry? Upset?"

"I am pissed." I retorted as I shifted in my seat, crossing my arms.

"Pissed? Because she chose someone else?"

"No, it's not that. I am pissed because I never asked for it."

"You both made decisions to spend time together, to be intimate. Is that not correct?"

I knew Ainsley wasn't to blame for what happened. There was no denying we connected mutually. Her friendship was something that had carried me through Dad's journey, but under scrutiny, I felt the need to divert responsibility. "I was vulnerable."

There was a moment of silence as he wrote something on his notepad before he cleared his throat. "Finn, what I think has happened here is you developed a very genuine connection with someone which I don't think, from what I know based on our history, you've had before. Now, that can often be a scary thing, feeling in a position of vulnerability. While you can't change what has happened, you now have the choice to accept that it has. We all make mistakes in life. It's a given as we navigate our journey. Would I call what has happened a mistake? Absolutely not. What I would call it though, is an experience which you can choose to take its lessons onto the next chapter in your life." He took a sip of water, studying me for a moment. "When I first met you, you were a very broken man. A lot of things had happened that you weren't in control of over there. You were a man who carried a lot of guilt and we really did some work on that, didn't we? We must have as here you are now, in a position of guilt and you are accepting there is an issue."

I nodded, unsure how to reply.

"I want to know, Finn, what do you feel is holding you back from letting this go?"

I froze, holding my breath for a moment. I asked myself that very question multiple times but could never find an answer I was fully certain of. Part of me knew it was because I let myself stick to a promise I made to myself when I was just a kid. Part of me knew it was because I missed her and I realised I had made a mistake. Part of me felt jealous because she found another who made her happy when I experienced nothing remotely close to what we shared. "I don't know." I said with a shrug.

"I think you know, deep in that brain of yours."

I gulped, feeling the flames of his scrutiny at my feet.

"I, well, I guess it is because I feel I made a mistake. It was the same mistake I made with my mother thinking there was time and we ended up losing that time because I couldn't get my shit together. Again, I made a mistake with my father, not recognising how sick he was until it was too late. I..." I froze, feeling the words heavy in my throat. "I made a mistake here, because I couldn't see what was right in front of me 'til it was too late."

He drew a deep breath, his face decorated with a slight smile.

"And there it is; acknowledgement. First things first, you prioritising yourself when you came home was highly important, Finn. You had a lot of things that needed addressing that will never be a mistake. A mistake is choosing to believe that. What happened with your father, you did not know of how bad things were because, as you put it, your mother hid so much. When it comes to this, you can accept it and take its lessons carrying them onto the next chapter of your life."

"What possible lessons can there be?" I stared at him with narrowed eyes.

"Well, if you ask me, I know this has been an issue for you. You can allow yourself to love another."

"I never said I loved her."

"You didn't need to." He stared at me, clearing his throat once more. "I don't know if you will recall when we first met, but you confessed to me several things. One being that you would never love anyone. Back then, I believed you. You were very defiant when I tried to convince you that committing yourself would limit your happiness; yet, here we are."

"Yes, here we are," I muttered.

"We can work through this Finn, and just like before, you will come out the other side."

It took a lot of work to modify behaviour over the course of the following year. I undertook a lot of cognitive and dialectical behavioural therapies. There were times I felt frustrated, as if I was back at square one, but slowly but surely I got my act together. With that came thoughts of the future because I had expressed to him I felt stuck. Dr Kent and I discussed many career options, but in the end, I felt the best option was to stay in the military until I was set with where I wanted to go next.

He told me it would get better, but it never did. Hours of therapy did little to help me accept my decision. In an effort to try my own therapy, I took Blair's advice. I went out with some of the younger guys in the battalion to a pub in the city's centre. Several pints later, I found myself in an unfamiliar apartment with a petite brunette whose name I couldn't remember.

While her name I cannot recollect, I can remember the way she kissed me and the way she tasted. She wasn't like Ainsley. Her body was different, her shape was different, and her scent was different. The way she touched me I didn't like, but in a primal manner, I took what I needed. When we were done, I knew I didn't want to stay. Instead, I got out of bed and got dressed. The urge to escape her was immense. She wasn't unattractive, and she seemed nice enough. I just couldn't feel any connection.

"Are you okay?" she asked, watching me as I got

dressed.

I couldn't look at her, feeling a taste of vomit against my lips. "I shouldn't be here," I replied, trying to find my shoe. "I shouldn't have come."

"It's a little late now," she said as she checked the time. "Just stay the night?"

"I have to go."

"Just like that? Really?"

"I'm sorry," I muttered before making my way to the door.

It became a decision I instantly regretted. As much as I wanted to have someone to talk to, it wasn't something I felt comfortable with. Whilst I had watched Blair mourn for several months when he and Michelle had separated, grieving a failed relationship wasn't something I felt was right. I had only known Ainsley for a short time, but for reasons I couldn't understand, I could not shake her. So I bit my tongue and hoped the feelings would disappear.

A week later, with the decision to stay enlisted set in stone, I once more found myself on the list to deploy, only this time in Iraq. I thought it would be a welcome distraction, but it only made the feelings worsen. With none of those that I had been enlisted with for so long alongside me, I found myself lost and confused without the familiarity of Blair or Colin at my disposal. Blair left and was set to take over his father's business as he became progressively unwell. Colin left mere months after we had returned from Afghanistan, unable to shake the ghosts we brought back with us.

Alone, listening to the sounds of rockets in the distance, my thoughts drifted to her. I wondered if she had built the life we likely could have had. Had she stayed in Aberdeen? Were she and Evan engaged? Married? It wasn't any of my business, but I couldn't help myself from entertaining the thoughts.

Fate or Fortune

Six months after my return from Iraq, Blair's father died after a brief battle with cancer. Given he had smoked a packet a day since we were children, it seemed inevitable that eventually his habits would have their effects.

The months I spent in the sand could have allowed for me to accept that Ainsley had moved on, and I could have too. I tried, but it was short-lived. I met a woman at work named Nina, who ironically bore a resemblance to Ainsley in build, skin tone and hair colour. I couldn't invest in her. My thoughts often wandered to Ainsley when we were together, which ultimately led to the demise of our love affair. It all came to a head after a night of drinking, when I accidentally called her Ainsley while we were getting hot and heavy in the kitchen.

"You are still in love with her," she hissed at me, throwing a glass from the counter which smashed into pieces on the floor. I will never forget the way she looked at me; her eyes infuriated but laced with sorrow. "Are you going to say anything, or should I just go?"

I stared at her, dumbfounded, knowing I should have fought for the situation, but the truth was I knew it was a road to nowhere. She wasn't *her*, and I only wanted *her*. I couldn't bring myself to stop Nina from leaving because I knew she was correct, and she deserved a chance at happiness. I would never be the one to give that to her.

As time passed, the days rolled into weeks and months. I questioned if I would ever come close to feeling what I felt with her ever again.

The morning of Blair's father's funeral, Blair and I went out for a breakfast of sausage, bacon and eggs at our local café and he could tell something was bothering me. We hadn't seen each other since I returned from Iraq, so it was the first time we had been in each other's presence for over two years.

"What's wrong with ye?" He took a bite of his sausage.

"Me?" I questioned, trying to sound convincing.

"You still love her, don't you?"

I kept my expression steady, but he read me anyway.

"It's okay," he said. "I already know. I've always known." He looked wistful. "I can still remember your face the first time I met her. I'd never seen you like that. I was happy for you because there was something about her I trusted right away."

"She met someone else."

"So did you, I heard." He quirked his eyebrows, chewing a mouthful of breakfast.

"Wasn't to be. Only lasted three months."

"There will be others."

I shook my head, cutting the egg on my plate, smearing it onto the bread. "I think I am done. At least for the time being."

"Nothing wrong with that."

"How about you? Everything going well with Shell?"

"Aye, things are going good. Looking to try for a baby after Christmas."

Blair and Michelle had patched things up and worked on setting healthy boundaries, which made them flourish. Even though I struggled to see the attraction in her outrageously sarcastic demeanour and intensity, I could see how much they had both grown. That was clear in how happy Blair was.

"That's great news."

"Aye, scary thought though."

We were in our mid-thirties, and it seemed everyone else had their families and were settled into lives of marriage and long partnerships. With Blair and Michelle looking to start a family, it was just me, becoming familiar with the sparse grey hairs and balding pattern making itself known in my hairline.

My mother always talked about fate – something I used to scoff at – but as if life had known we were discussing Ainsley that morning, she appeared, seated two tables across from us. Alone.

"Finn," Blair hissed, realising it was her before I did.

"What?"

He widened his eyes, scrutinising her. "Would you look at that?"

I took a sip of my tea, shooting my eyes past him briefly to view her. I wouldn't dare give Blair the satisfaction of anything more than a three second glance.

Blair quizzed as he grinned wider than a Cheshire cat. "Are you going to go say hi?"

"Of course, I will not bloody say hello." I replied, nearly spitting my tea out.

"Why not?"

"Because, why would I?"

"Seize the opportunity maybe?" Blair said, his smile fixed.

Willing myself not to look at her again, I insisted, "there is no opportunity. That ship has sailed."

"Perhaps not. You won't know unless you talk to her."

"Can ye just put a sock in it? I'm not talking to her."

"Well, Finny, I think you are going to have to. She's walking over here."

I stared at him, trying to establish whether he was having a laugh. A conclusion was drawn when I heard Ainsley's familiar voice behind me. "Hey there, you two."

I turned around slowly, meeting her gaze to see her deep auburn hair was dyed a light strawberry blonde, cut just below her jawline. A vast change from the long, wavy, intriguing red locks I had once known.

"I like the hair," Blair quipped. "How have you been?"

She pulled the chair out from next to me, taking a seat. Distanced enough so our forearms lightly brushed. "I needed a change." She laughed, running her hands through her hair. "I have been really great; busy, you know? Life. How about you?" She directed the question at Blair as I sat uncomfortably, unsure where to look.

"Well, my old Dad, he passed away. That's why this one..." Blair replied as he gave me a kick from under the table, causing it to jolt. "That is why this one is here."

Ainsley turned back to face me, making eye contact so I couldn't turn away. "Well, it is nice to see you back in your neighbourhood." She smiled. I sensed it was genuine, giving the small creases that formed in an upward line where her lip met her cheek. She held my gaze for a moment before turning her attention back to Blair. "I'm sorry to hear that, I truly am."

"It's okay. His own doing. Loved his fags too much," Blair laughed, shooting me a wide-eyed stare. "Tell ye what, you two have some catching up to do so I will go and square up."

Before I could stop him, he excused himself, leaving Ainsley and me sitting in an awkward silence.

"Subtlety is not his strong point." I laughed nervously in an effort to break the ice.

"You're right," she giggled in reply. I missed that sound and it wasn't any less sweet after all these years.

"So, how are you? How is life in Edinburgh?"

"It's fine, I guess. Same old, same old. What about you?"

She smiled, signalling to the waiter scanning the tables looking for her. "Well, me and Evan broke up, but life is good. Work has been good, actually. Would you believe I got a promotion?"

"A promotion?" I ignored her revelation about a man I despised even though I didn't know who he was.

She smiled at the server as her meal was placed in front of her. "I'm the charge nurse now."

"That is great. I am happy for you."

"How long are you here for?" She sipped her coffee.

"Maybe a week. I need to organise selling my flat. It's been empty for two years. Probably about time."

She paused, deep in thought. "How much are you selling it for?"

"Do you know someone who is looking to buy?"

"Well, yes, me."

For the first time, I looked at her, really taking in all her features. She hadn't aged at all, minus a few faint crease lines appearing in the corners of her eyes. "Ainsley..."

"Finn, I'm serious. I have been looking for quite some time but nothing has felt right."

"Do you even remember what the flat looks like?"

She let out a nervous laugh, picking at the handle on her mug. "Do you want to get a drink?" she asked, evading the question.

I looked past her, seeing Blair talking on his phone, shooting periodic glances in our direction. "Sure, when?"

"What about tonight?"

"Tonight?" I was surprised by her urgency.

"I have night shifts the rest of the week."

"Okay, well tonight then. Should I pick you up?"

"No, that would make it a date," she said, smirking at the inside joke.

"And it's not?" I joked.

"Well, I'm undecided on that." We both laughed. It was something that had become foreign, the very sensation of joy, but in her presence I couldn't help myself. "Well, I'll see you later, then." She smiled, bringing herself to a stand.

"Aye, see you later."

∞∞∞∞

Making our way back to Blair's family home to organise ourselves for the service, he couldn't prevent the intrigue from escaping his lips. "So, what happened?"

"Nothing happened," I replied defensively.

"Something. I can tell just by looking at you."

I let out a sigh, aware that he knew me too well. "We are going out for dinner."

"A date?" Blair questioned, grinning.

"Not a date."

"Sounds like a date," Blair laughed as we stopped at a red light.

"Can two friends not go out for a nice, friendly meal without their being a motive behind it?"

"Aye, they can but not two friends that look at each

other the way you two do."

I stared out the window, clueless to a reply, watching a couple walking their dog on the sidewalk. "How are you feeling about today?" I questioned to change the subject.

Blair gave me a sideways glance. "Finny, don't do that."

"Do what?"

"Change the subject."

"What more do you want me to say?"

"Don't mess it up is all I am going to say. You have one chance at this. She is a catch. Smart, gorgeous and she likes you and that is saying something. She is either daft or sees something in you."

I reflected on a conversation my mother and I had just before I left for the army at sixteen. "People come into your life for a reason, a season or a lifetime, Finn," she said as she stirred the pot of casserole on the stove top. "I want you to always know that because not everyone comes into your life to stay."

At sixteen, I couldn't comprehend what she meant, but in my mid-thirties, the concept was easier to understand.

People had come into my life for several reasons. They had left, and I had often uncovered the lesson of their existence weeks and sometimes years later. Those that had come into my life for a season helped me through a period of growth when I needed it and we went our separate ways. My mother always said a lifetime love teaches you lifetime lessons, and I had learnt more about myself in the time I had known Ainsley than I had my entire life.

Our friendship was so natural; one that never felt forced or felt an effort to maintain. My parents' foundation had always been built on friendship, one where they navigated the seas of life as a team. Through life's trials and triumphs, sometimes they had not necessarily liked each other, but they had always loved each other. Reflecting on Blair's words, I knew it was clear she loved me in not just what she said but her actions. I wanted to love her, but a part of me still felt that nagging fear that I would lose her. Whether through life's actions or our own, I still was not convinced that the fear of that trumped my desire to be with her.

Reflection

My aversion to love was not just bound to people, I struggled to grow affections for anything. When I was eight years old, for Christmas, my father bought my mother a black cocker spaniel dog she called Georgie.

For my mother, she loved him like he was a child of hers, but for me, I found myself hesitant to even touch him. My mother became so concerned over the matter that she eventually made me see a child psychologist named Dr Maxwell.

Sitting in the waiting room in silence, I remember my mother nervously fiddling with the trim of her skirt. "Finn, my sweet boy, remember what we spoke about in the car," she whispered, giving my hand a tight squeeze. The whole fifteen-minute car ride, my mother, in her heightened state of worry, reiterated the importance of honesty, as if I didn't understand the meaning of it. "Finn, this man is here to help you, so don't feel you cannot be honest with him," she said for a third time, albeit in a different dialogue.

I nodded, staring out the window, wishing for it all to be over.

Mr Maxwell, a short time later, came and got us from the waiting room, dressed in deep green khaki-coloured pants and a white linen dress shirt. He was a George Clooney doppelganger. "Finn," he said, bending down to meet my stature. "Hi Finn, my name is Dr Maxwell." He warmly smiled before standing and shaking my mother's hand. "Come through."

Mr Maxwell's office was the third down the hallway to the right, adorned with pictures of wildlife and sea creatures. It brought a sense of calm to a situation that felt overwhelming.

"Take a seat," he said, smiling. "Tell me what is going on."

My mother was first, nervously glancing at me. "I am concerned about Finn. He has become increasingly unaffectionate. His teacher Mrs Robinson has expressed she has concerned about his emotional demeanour lacking variety."

"Explain that to me," Mr Maxwell questioned, jotting on a notepad.

"Well, she said he never seems happy nor sad."

"And do you experience the same?"

My mother paused, her voice trembling. "Yes, no, I mean I guess so."

"Does he have friends?"

"A few."

"And what is his relationship like with them?"

"Good, I think. They are always out doing things in the neighbourhood."

Mr Maxwell paused from his writing, glancing at me.

"Would you mind if I talk to Finn in private?"

"Of course not," my mother said as she stood. "I will wait in the waiting room."

I watched as my mother disappeared out of view down the hallway before fixating on a picture of two lions to the right of the door, feeling at unease.

"Finn, I am going to ask you a few questions, okay?" Mr Maxwell said softly. I turned to face him, nodding as he scanned his desk for a piece of paper. "Your mother said she is concerned that you don't seem interested in your pet dog anymore, Georgie?"

I nodded again, picking at my hands.

"Tell me, why is that?"

I shrugged, looking at him blankly. What did he expect me to say? I was only a child.

"What colour is he?" He tried a different approach.

"Black."

"Do you like playing with him?"

I nodded.

"What is his favourite game?"

"He likes it when I throw his ball."

"Do you like throwing the ball for him?"

I nodded again.

"So Finn, why does your mum tell me you don't enjoy touching him or letting him sleep with you." He stared at me intensely, clicking his pen against the desk. The truth was, what had always been a case, I didn't want to care about him, to only then lose him.

"I don't want him to be my friend."

"Why is that?" He questioned.

I paused, staring at him. "Because I don't want to lose him if he is my friend."

Dr Maxwell looked at me, surprised, writing on his notepad again. "Why would you lose him?"

"Because everything has to die."

Mr Maxwell placed his pen down, running his hands through his stubble. "Does it scare you, Finn? The thought of those you care about dying?"

I could feel my heart pounding in my chest from nerves, unable to reply, so I nodded again.

"That is quite a normal thing."

"Why does it happen though?" I asked, the words escaped my lips. I had occasionally asked my parents why Lyall had died, but it was never something they told me. I felt Dr Maxwell would give me a more satisfying answer.

"Well, Finn, that is part of life. We shouldn't fear it and view it as part of living. We aren't meant to live forever."

"But why, if it makes people sad?"

"Well Finn, it is normal to be sad when we lose the ones we love. Eventually it gets better."

"But my mother, she still cries for my brother. So does my dad, but he goes away in the car to cry."

"Your brother?"

"My brother died when I was little."

"Did he?" He questioned, the tone in his voice reflecting his concern.

"Yes. I don't really remember him though."

"What was his name? Do you remember?"

"Lyall."

He paused, reading a piece of paper from a bright yellow manila folder. "I see. How does it make you feel, Finn? That you lost your brother?"

I paused, feeling my heart rapidly in my chest. Nobody had asked me these questions before. "Well, I don't enjoy seeing my mother sad. She hides in the bathroom, but I can still hear her from my room."

Dr Maxwell placed the piece of paper down, running his hands through the sparse stubble on his chin. "And your father? Where is he?"

"My dad is at sea," I replied. "He is in the navy."

"I see," he replied, fiddling with a paperweight on his desk. There was a moment's pause as he stared at me directly, which made me feel flustered. "Finn, I am going to talk to your mum for a wee bit, okay? If you sit in the waiting room, we won't be long."

I will never know what he said behind closed doors, but from that day onward I never saw or heard my mother cry again and I never saw Dr Maxwell again either. Things changed shortly after that visit. I came home from school to find all pictures of Lyall had been removed from the house, including the one that served as a fond memory, us four seated outside a large oak on the shores of the loch. They stopped talking about him altogether where once upon a time they would refer to him in a memory of a reflective thought about something he enjoyed.

The change made me feel uncomfortable, as if the grief had to be served as a secret; one that we should never display outwardly as if I was expected to forget he existed. Something changed within my mother too as I made the mistake of accidentally referring to him in a sentence, unaware of the ramifications.

Mrs Robinson had just had a baby, and she called him Lyall. She had visited us at school and I remember coming home excited to tell my parents about the new baby. My mother was in the kitchen getting herself organised for her night shift at work, tying her hair up in the mirror of the buffet cabinet.

"Mum, guess what?" I said cheerfully.

"What?" she replied, smiling as she straightened her bun.

"Mrs Robinson had a baby, and she called him Lyall too."

I watched as my mother's face froze before she pushed past me and made her way upstairs.

My father, having returned from the sea two weeks prior, was sitting at the dining room table having a cup of tea and scones, let out a sigh. "Ignore that Finny, she will be okay."

I stared at him, confused, as we both jolted from the sound of the door upstairs slamming. "What did I do?"

My father paused, running his tongue over his lips. "You did nothing Finn, your ma, she can get like this."

It became a common occurrence; one I didn't have the maturity to understand until I was older. I would often sit in my bed cradling one of my stuffed animals, confused by what I had done, unable to rationalise the cause of her outbursts. I watched as the years went on and it never went away. Eventually declaring to myself I would never allow myself to have children or love if it meant there was a possibility I would turn into her. She never could let it go. Hidden in her denial and inability to be reminded of him was a woman who simply could not forget. My father, in his own way, battled the same feelings. Meetings alone to grieve in private and hours spent sitting on a rock peering out at the ocean. Unlike my mother, my father accepted my curiosity to talk about him, but the more self-aware I became about the effect it had on my mother, the less I did.

Blair would often refer to me as the lamppost, one who showed nothing other than neutrality. It wasn't as if I didn't experience happiness or sadness, but the ability to express that became suppressed in the fear it would upset her. This made me a good soldier because I could stay rational when there were times that everything was chaotic. The problem was, as a consequence, my interpersonal relationships suffered.

I had several casual flings before Brianna, but she was the first when its prevalence was made known. After we had been dating for close to a year, we had gone to her parents' holiday home. She had come from a family of wealth with her father, a university lecturer, and her mother working in criminal law. I never understood why she had joined the military, but I wondered if it was an act driven by defiance.

She had been dropping hints for quite some time she had wanted to make things official, but each time I found an ability to sweep it under the rug. The evening started off well where we had gone out for dinner, having a few drinks with our meal, and by the time we got back to the house, we were both a bit tiddly.

"Do you love me?" Brianna said, sitting herself on top of the kitchen counter taking off her shoes.

I looked at her, bursting out laughing at her question. "What do you mean, do I love you? We haven't been together very long?"

"Finn, we have been seeing each other for a year." She shook her head, sliding down from the counter. "I don't know why you are like this."

"Like what?"

"This," she said fiercely, gesturing with her hands. "You are never anything, Finn. I don't know if you are hot or cold. You barely kiss me unless you want to fuck and even then it feels forced. I see you in glimpses, but it is never consistent, mainly when you have been drinking. It seems to be the only thing that takes the veil off you, allowing me to see you, really see you. Finn, I just want you to love me. I have tried and I don't know what more I can do. Why don't you love me? Why can't you love me?"

I stared at her, frozen, unsure of what to say. I knew I didn't love her because her words didn't fill me with a concern like I thought they would.

"Why can't you love me? Is there someone else?"

"No, of course there's not," I retorted.

"Then what is it?"

"I just can't. I can't be who you need me to be" I shrugged, watching as she picked up her shoes. For a second I thought she was going to throw them in my direction, but she instead walked over to the door, placing them down on the rack.

"You will never be loved, Finn, if this is how you are going to be. It's over."

I never dwelled on it and, even though I didn't want to hurt her, I knew I had. On the two occasions I saw her after our breakup, there was an intensity about her longing to see an emotion from me proving I did care about her. Brianna was a likeable girl, and we had fun. Even now I question if I had forgotten my oath to myself, would I have been able to love her? The thing was, I didn't know how. I was immature. I had for so long run from the prospect that even if I had given myself a chance to love her, I don't think I ever fully could. Faced with the situation again, I knew something had to change or the result would be the same.

Calm

The afternoon before I was to meet Ainsley, I went and visited my mother, taking a fresh bunch of tulips with me.

I hadn't been back there for years and as I stared at her unkempt stone becoming covered in moss, I felt a wave of guilt. "I'm sorry Ma," I whispered as I swept the blanket of leaves off. "I hope you are having a blast up there," I said as I tilted my head to the grey sky. "Both of you."

I sat for a while, telling them I hoped to leave the army soon. After spending close to two decades enlisted, I no longer felt it was right for me. All the faces around me felt foreign, and I needed change. While I wasn't certain what I wanted to do, I knew it would be something that supported people.

"I guess that is you coming out in me, Ma," I said out loud with a laugh. I glanced at my watch, realising I needed to get organised, and said my goodbyes. "I will come back before I head home, Ma," I said, giving her stone one last sweep.

Ainsley and I had agreed in a text message exchange to meet at the very place we had gone on our first date, even if she refused to admit it was a date. When I arrived, she was waiting outside in the cool early winter air, watching patrons pass her on the street. Dressed in a fitted red dress and black coat with her hair loose, I couldn't help my breath from quickening as I approached.

"They have no tables, at least not for an hour or two," she said as I walked towards her.

"Somewhere else then? Come, we can try my dad's favorite ol' place. It's not far."

A few blocks away, there was an underground pub my father loved visiting. It was rough around the edges, but inside their food was some of the best in Aberdeen.

"Okay," she replied with a hesitant grin. "Lead the way."

As we walked, there was a tense silence. Ainsley kept her head low, fixating on the footpath broken by occasional glances in my direction.

"Where is this place?" she finally asked.

"Just a little farther," I said. "Up there, at the end."

"It's kind of out of the way, isn't it?"

"Well, yes, I suppose. It's kind of a local institution, though, so it doesn't matter," I said. A minute later, I slowed, and we turned into the small home-style pub at the bottom of a six-story apartment complex.

"Well, this is different," Ainsley remarked, unsure of what to make of its run down, unkempt appearance.

I wondered whether I should reach for her hand, but in the end I did nothing. "You ready?"

"As I'll ever be," she joked, and I pushed open the

door.

I don't know what she expected, but she wore a satisfied expression as she stepped inside. Hidden inside was a rustic bar with a line of half a dozen booths to the right. The air held the greasy smell of fried food and cigarette smoke, but somehow it seemed just right. Most of the tables were filled, but I motioned towards one waiting to be cleared to the left of the bar.

"I like places like this," she said, taking a seat. "They remind me of home. Was this you and your father's regular hangout?"

"No, this was more of a special-occasion place."

"I see. Well… "She reached for a laminated menu sandwiched standing up right in its holder. "What's this place famous for?"

"You will laugh if I tell you."

"Haggis?"

I shook my head. "Close, but it has the best, and I mean best, bangers and mash," I said with a laugh.

"Gee, really?" She couldn't help but laugh. "Well, that is –"

"Tempting?"

"I wouldn't say tempting is the word," she said, her voice dripping with sarcasm.

The waitress showed up, and I ordered my father's usual pork bangers and mash with a side of potato.

"Make it two," Ainsley added.

After the waitress left, we settled into easy conversation, uninterrupted even when our food arrived. We talked about life, what had happened since we had last seen each other.

"These sausages, I mean, wow. You weren't wrong." She said, smiling as she cut another piece of her gravy smeared sausages.

"I told you, pretty much famous around these parts."

I couldn't help but listen intently as she talked about work, asking questions now and then. Observing her ignited the flame of just how much I enjoyed being alone with her. I wanted to see more of her, have her in my life. Not just tonight, but tomorrow and the next day. Then again, spending time with her that evening also made me realise how lonely I'd been. I hadn't admitted that to myself, but an hour into dinner with Ainsley, I knew it was true.

Once our plates were finished, we sat across from each other in silence. Ainsley scowled slightly, resting her head in her palm. "I think you know this question is coming," she whispered, biting her lip.

"What question?" I queried.

"Why did you end things the way you did?"

"How else was I meant to?"

"I don't know," she replied with a shrug. "I guess I hoped you would fight for me."

"You told me you were happy?" I replied, somewhat irritated by her assumption. If I had thought her revelation all those years ago was merely a fling, of course, I would have fought for her. It was by her own admission that she was happy, ultimately picking his feelings over my own why I didn't.

"You are right; I'm sorry."

"It's in the past. Do you want to tell me what happened?"

"What happened?"

"To you and Evan?"

She pursed her lips, as if to question her answer. "He knew."

"He knew what? About us?"

"Oh God no, Finn." She leaned forward to grab a napkin, wiping the corners of her mouth. "He knew I didn't love him. Certainly not the way I loved you."

"You did though?" I was curious.

"I did what?" She questioned, her voice sounded annoyed.

"Love him?" It was none of my business, but I felt a strong desire to know if she had allowed herself the liberty when I had struggled to do the same.

Ainsley paused, staring at me with a startled expression, as if she was unsure of how to reply without causing offence. "No, I mean, I cared about him, Finn. I wanted to love him, but I couldn't." I nodded, unsure what to say as Ainsley picked nervously at her used napkin. "He was a good man Finn, he just... Well... He just wasn't you."

I swallowed. "When can I see you again?"

It was a simple question, expected even, but I was surprised to hear the notable desire in my tone.

"I suppose," she said with a smirk, "that depends on you. You know where I am."

We made our way outside, heading back to our vehicles. For a moment, we stood in one of those awkward moments where neither knows what to say. I wanted her, but she turned away before I could attempt a kiss to let that be known. In our past life, I would have plunged ahead just to see what happened. I may not have been open about my feelings, but I was impulsive and quick to action. That night, I felt oddly paralyzed.

"Thank you for tonight," she said, bringing me in for a brief hug. "If you would like to, I would love to do this again before you head back. When do you go home?"

"Sometime next week," I replied, glancing over her shoulder at a couple engaged in a heavily intoxicated argument.

She smiled. "Don't forget I want to see this apartment, too."

"We can organise that," I replied, digging my hands into my jacket pocket.

"Okay, cool. I look forward to that." She looked down at her feet nervously and I could sense we were both thinking the same thing.

"How about now?" I questioned, my voice nervous.

"Now?"

"Aye. We can have a cuppa on the terrace."

"All right, let's do it."

The journey back to the apartment was just four blocks but the whole time we walked in silence. I wanted to invade her thoughts, wanted to know what she was thinking, but she gave nothing away from her neutral expression.

When we got inside, she slid off her coat, studying the walls decorated with artwork my mother had periodically painted when time allowed.

"Who painted these?" she questioned, walking over towards a painting of Barns Ness Lighthouse.

"My mother did."

"Wow," she remarked, studying it intently.

"She did all of them," I replied, standing back as I observed her.

"Finn..." Ainsley turned to face me. "I need to know."

"Need to know what?"

"Why did you run? Why are we standing here all these years later? Are we friends? Are we not friends? I am asking myself all those questions right now, the very same questions I asked myself back then."

"Of course, we are friends. Would I be here if we weren't?"

She didn't answer. Instead, she looked away, wiped her face and walked herself to the lounge, where she dropped herself onto the couch. "No."

"I'm sorry," I muttered under my breath as I walked over to her and taking a seat next to her.

"What do you want, Finn?" She leaned forward, her hands pulled to her face. "It doesn't have to be like this, you realise?"

"I know," I muttered.

Tears filled her eyes. "Then what is it?" she whispered.

I could feel the words on the tip of my tongue waiting to escape.

"Finn, please answer me!"

"Ainsley, I..." I shook my head, glancing at her briefly. "I... I don't want to love someone and lose them and I... Well, I guess I knew you loved you. I loved you then, just as I do now."

"Wait, you love me?"

I held her gaze, my eyes moist.

"Of course I do, but I accepted I had to let you go."

There was a silence and all I could hear was her nervous, rapid breaths. After a moment, she gently turned me towards her, placing her hands on my own. "Oh, Finn," she said as the tears began again. "You won't lose me."

I shook my head to stop her. "I know what you're trying to say. I can see it in your eyes. But you don't want to understand it; it isn't something anyone can control."

She paused in reflection of my words, trying to piece them together. "Finn, nobody can promise that, but do you know what I can promise? I can promise I will love you every single part of you, even the parts you don't think are loveable. I will love them. My life was never the same since you left and I won't lose you again, I..." She paused, taking a deep trembling breath. "I won't lose you again. I can't."

I froze. I realized in that moment that loss can happen whether you love someone up close or from a distance. By pushing Ainsley away, I was still losing what I loved. Something overtook me and I gave in to it, hoping it would take us back to all we had felt a lifetime ago. I pulled her closer, intoxicating myself in her. I gave in to everything I had fought against for the last two years. Ainsley lifted her gaze to look at me, and I kissed her softly on the lips. She brought her hand to my face and ran her smooth fingers across the stubble on my cheek. I paused before I leaned in and kissed her tenderly, and she kissed me back, feeling the years of separation dissolve all at once.

Epilogue

Ainsley

When I saw the signs in him, for I had worked for most of my career seeing the faces of the illness that had cut lives too short in the cruellest of ways. When I arrive, he is staring out the window, lost in his own world, I try to comfort myself knowing that he may not remember that I have been.

"Hello my dear," I whisper as I sit down next to him on the bed. Even though he had aged, the lines on his face cut like ravens in a canyon, the very sight of his mischievous smile made my heart quiver.

To love another like he loved me, I knew, was a rarity in life. Some spend their whole lives searching for a love like ours and I found it in a place I never expected I would.

He looked me in the eyes, and for a moment, I saw the softest glimmer in him. A spark of recognition that assures me he is still there, even if who he was is not. A slight smile forms on his lips. "You again."

I smile, realising today at least his humour remained. "I read once, persistence is everything."

"You were always so determined," he smiles as he

brings his hand to my face.

We sit quietly for a while, watching as the world continues on around us. Our two children have gone on to have successful lives. Our son joined the military, just like his father. Our daughter became a paediatric nurse, just like her grandmother. Finn may not remember in great detail the life that we lived, but I do.

Our life was one I never thought I would ever have.

A year after we decided to make a go of it, we travelled, eventually settling in Ireland. Finn, at thirty-five, decided he was going to study in the medical field psychology to help better the understanding of post-traumatic stress in soldiers. We got the house, a small farmlet in a village on the outskirts of Dublin. It wasn't without its difficulties, the inevitable journey of life, but for the most part, life was all I could have wanted and more.

He is deteriorating fast. I know my time will be shorter than either of us would have liked. He has become afraid of the dark again, after spending years of his life trying to overcome that. There are days when I visit when he cries inconsolably when he recognises that the familiar foe has come for him too. While I am able to make sure he is clean, he has started to not eat regularly. The man I once knew is wasting away, becoming more frail with each passing day.

But for today, he is here with me, and for that, I am

Grateful.

Acknowledgement

I would like to thank both Michelle and Tiffany for assisting me with this book. None of this would have been possible without the unlimited support and guidance you gave me to complete this project.

About The Author

Harriet Pearce

Harriet resides in New Zealand with her partner and children.

Born with a passion for story telling it wasn't until she reached her thirties that she decided it was something worth persuing.

Passionate about mental health, she is currently studying Mental Health and Addiction at University.

She has a number of previous titles the novellas 'Sunhsine After The Rain' and 'After The Storm' as well as her Inivsible War Series which centres around military mental health.

She looks forward to sharing her stories about people, for people to have a better understanding of our world.

Printed in Great Britain
by Amazon

75095160R00159